Slow to Anger

SHAIDA ESCOFFERY WHITLEY

DEDICATION

To Micah. I love you.

CONTENTS

ACKNOWLEDGMENTS

It's been seven years since my last publication, and it's been a long journey. There have been plenty of moments of self-doubt. I just want to say thank you to my family for walking with me through those moments and encouraging me to still produce another novel.

Thank you to Victoria Castells, for taking the time to be an early reader of my manuscript. Your encouragement and feedback were invaluable.

Thank you to my church family and friends. Everything from here on out, is for the kingdom and for his glory.

Azariah
TENNESSEE
1805

"Prophets don't have no choice," they always said to me, "You jus' born that way". God made Jeremiah a prophet before he was even born. God tell 'em what to say and where to go. They ain't got no choice but to obey God and be his mouth to the people. Pa always told me that he felt that I had some special purpose when I was born. He said that I came out feet first and lived. When he saw me for the first time, he instantly remembered a scripture someone had told him long ago, "How beautiful are the feet of those who bring good tidings". I was born to bring the good news. He said my mom told him he was thinking too highly and then when I was 10 years old, Master Arthur Marshall told him that I was gon' be the next preacher for the rest of the slaves in all the farms and plantations round here.

"God don't make no mistakes," he said to me when Master Marshall gave permission for me to learn to read so that I could start training. Our weatherworn, one room, wooden cabin was just like every other wooden cabin where the slaves lived, but ours was different. It had a larger porch. I never noticed this, but other children around the plantation would tell me that Master Marshall gave my mom a big 'ol porch because my mother, Venus, was a loose woman. I'm sure that they heard this from their own mothers. I didn't understand that at the time. What did it mean to be a loose woman? But I could sense the insult in their voice, and I remember the heat that flooded my body before I had struck one of the boys, over and over again. I nearly received a lashing for that, but again, my mother had convinced Master Marshall to spare me. Master Marshall called her Venus, and she had to respond to it, but my mother's given name was Zuri. It was given to her by her grandmother who still spoke their original Mandinka language. Sometimes my mother still said words or phrases here and there, like when she would tell me that she loved me. *Nye kanu laye.* I also always knew the knew the word for home. *Kunda.* Sometimes, I imitated her by speaking quickly and singing songs in the same melody, but most times I ended speaking gibberish. She would smile with amusement, but she never went through too much trouble to teach me any words. I often wonder if it was because she knew that her access to the language was so limited. Besides, Master Marshall didn't like talk that sounded too African, she told me.

"He would think we were up to somethin'."

In fact, anyone who had a name that sounded too African had their name changed around here. Calling someone by their African name could be punished, so Pa made sure to only call Mama "Zuri" when we were at home. Master Marshall had always seemed like a large looming figure. He was a tall man with blond hair that he kept neatly cut and combed back from his face underneath his hat. The only time he took it off was in the house, because Mrs. Marshall didn't tolerate hats in the house. However, he always wore his tan one outside. He loved wearing nice hats and suits because he was the top businessman in the region. It didn't really make sense for him to be walking around in the Tennessee heat with all of us, but he just could never give over full trust and control to his overseers, and he simultaneously could not part with his fancy taste. So, the women on the plantation hands were dry, cracked, and sometimes red and raw from working with lye to keep the Marshall family's clothing clean.

People often came to his sprawling white estate, with its tall white columns, complete with a brick sugar mill and ten acres of fields white with cotton. Mrs. Marshall called the place Red Oaks because of the trees that surrounded the place. During the autumn months, the place looked like it had been set ablaze by all the red leaves that sprung up, but Master Marshall, in his self-importance, insisted that the place be called The Marshall Plantation.

Master Marshall had always watched me with a keen eye, and I couldn't tell if it was because he thought there was something different or special about me or if he meant to beat or sell me, so I feared him. Hearing that he wanted me to train to be the next preacher was a shock for me. It changed our cabin forever. Instead of just our slightly larger porch being the only difference between us and the rest of the slaves, for years ours was the only cabin where reading took place. It was the only cabin where along with the sounds of birds chirping in the morning, or crickets chirping at night, you could faintly hear someone sounding out vowels. It was the only cabin where sunlight penetrated through the trees and the refraction from our window was used to illuminate words on pages and whereby candlelight, I sought to understand what these words meant. All my life I had never questioned my father's words, but when I finally started to read; "God don't make no mistakes", started to sound like a lie.

***

Master Marshall went to church more than the pastor himself but didn't have any problem taking the whip from the overseers themselves to handle a slave that was falling out of line. You could be outta line for a whole lot of things according to Master Marshall: picking too slow, picking too fast so that you can have the rest of the day off, having another comment besides "yes suh", "no suh", "yes ma'am", and "no ma'am", and for looking him dead in the eye.

Pa told me that Master Marshall purchased him when he was just a teenager. He had been split from his family in Louisiana and moved here to Tennessee. When he was brought here to

The Marshall Plantation, he was determined to keep his head low and not cause any problems. Also, he vowed not to marry and have babies that he might be separated from. He said his own pa and sister had been sold to another farm, and he often woke up in the middle of the night crying the name of his only known family left on that plantation, his mother, Ruth. My father was notorious for having nightmares. His big body would often thrash in the night as he made unintelligible cries and yells. His almond-colored skin would be slick with sweat. Once, I asked him what he dreamt about. His only response to me had been, "Some things ain't to be shared. Some things hurt too bad and are too scary."

"I ain't gonna get scared," I said to him.

He hung his head, and I almost didn't hear what he said. "You'll feel what I feel."

Pa never told me, but once when my parents thought I was asleep, they lay whispering about my fate working under Master Marshall.

"Daniel, what that man want with Azariah?" Mama whispered. I could imagine her fair skin and her loose curls, always tied tightly at the nape in a bun, when she was working at the big house. At home, her hair was a wild splay of curls that puffed and spiraled.

"He wants him to learn to read the Bible. Want him to be the next preacher once he grows up."

"Why?"

"Zuri, what I'm supposed to know that for? Master Marshall say he wants Azariah to learn. I ain't got nothing to say to that but yes. He light. Master Reeves across the way say he look white. He said it'll keep the rest of us in line."

My mouth had dropped open, and I closed it and tried to keep my breathing even, not to draw their suspicion.

Mama whispered back vehemently, "What you think he's gon' do to keep Azariah in line? You think he's gonna mess with the boys like they did where you came from? I ain't gonna have that happen to mine!"

"And you think I'm gonna have it happen

to mine?"

The breeze blew hard outside, and a tree branch scratched against the cabin. I heard someone rustle up off the floor. I recognized my Pa's heavy footsteps. "I told you, I don't ever wanna talk about that. Ever." The only sounds in our cabin that remained were the sounds of the night.

****

The next morning, I remember that as soon as the sun was up, Pa walked with me over to the church, and there was Master Marshall and another plantation owner called Mr. Reeves waiting for us outside the door. Mr. Reeves had a reputation of being a real soft slave owner. His slaves didn't get beat, and they seemed to still stay in line and everything. People from my plantation would often say amongst themselves that they'd love to get sold to Mr. Reeves' farm. But he didn't have as many slaves working under him as Master Marshall did, so until one of his slaves got sick and died, there was no chance of getting purchased by Mr. Reeves. Marshall's plantation was much different: we all had different tasks, whether that was cotton picking, working at the Big House, or working in the sugar mill. There was an overseer over every group, and we all had to live close to the Big House so that Master Marshall could have a close eye on us. Mr. Reeves was nothing like that it seemed. People moved about freely, I'd heard, and they were obedient. I'd always seen him from afar, but I had never been this close to him.

"This here's the boy, Azariah, that I told you about, Reeves," Mr. Marshall said curtly.

Mr. Reeves and Master Marshall were like night and day. Both were clean-shaven men who seemed to take pride in their appearance, but where Master Marshall's hair was light, Mr. Reeves had such dark hair, it appeared to be black to me. He wore dark clothing even though it was sweltering, his hair was combed neatly on his head, and although he was pale, he wore no hat to shade himself from the sun. I wondered how he could keep from fainting in the heat or turning red like Master Marshall did when he was outside for too long. The more I got to know him, the more I realized that he was rarely outside for long. He stayed inside his study or the church. Master Marshall commanded me to come over to him, and I felt Pa's hand tighten on my shoulder for a slight second before he released me.

Master Marshall was wearing this light tan suit that was sure to get dirty and he wore his dark blond hair under his signature hat. "You see how high yella this boy here is?" he said laughing, but it didn't sound like the laugh my father gives whenever we play outside. It sounded like each chuckle was biting at me.

"Quite fair indeed," Reeves said, and it was then I noticed that he sounded funny. He didn't sound like any man from Tennessee that I'd ever known. "My Lord, he looks almost like my son," he said with shock, still staring down at me.

I saw Master Marshall's skin turn a slight

pink color, like an evening storm was building beneath his skin. "He's property, ain't nothing gonna change that, and it's best that he always remembers that, Reeves," he snapped, sternly looking at Mr. Reeves. "Ain't that right, Daniel?'

"Yessuh, that's right," Pa quickly responded as his fingers gripped his own hat tightly. I had heard the whispers about me and seen the cutting eyes of some of the other children whose skin tones ranged from almond to tree bark. But for the first time, I felt shame that my skin mirrored Master Marshall's, that my hair only had slightly more curl than Master Marshall's own son. I felt shame that I was not white, that I was "property" as Master Marshall said. But to everyone that lived amongst us, I was not a part of them either. I didn't belong anywhere, with anyone.

Mr. Reeves gave a small smile. "Marshall, I remind you, I've never had to beat not a one of mine, and they all remember their place. The mind must be broken first."

Master Marshall instantly relaxed into a

real laugh this time. "You one crazy fool, Reeves. You use your book to remind yours, and I'll use my whip, but this here ain't England nor the West Indies. You think you can rely on your book here? You best learn to use a whip, cause these slaves from Tennessee need constant reminding. Ain't that right, Daniel?"

My father had sweat now on the line between his tightly coiled blond hair, and it ran down, his sandy skin and into his hazel eyes. "Yessuh."

Master Marshall nodded towards my father. "Daniel seemed to have raised this boy well. He ain't never given no real trouble. Neither has his Pa, since coming to me. Used to give a whole lot of trouble back at his plantation over there in Louisiana but we fixed that problem when he got over here. Ain't that right, Daniel?"

"Yessuh, I don't give no mo' trouble, and Azariah ain't never giv'n no trouble and never will."

Master Marshall smiled widely. "Now

that's what I love to hear!" he said, raising his arms. Mr. Reeves gave a small smile, "I see why the society here reveres you, Marshall."

"Reeves, I don't understand half of what you say, but I'll take it as a compliment." He left me at Mr. Reeves' side and walked over to Pa. "Well, I'll leave you to it, Reeves. He'll be here first thing in the morning and every day I want him back on my plantation by sundown, or he'll have to get used to my way of remembrance. Understood?"

"Understood," Mr. Reeves confirmed, tipping his head. Then Master Marshall ordered my Pa to head back to the plantation. My dad gave me one last look of concern and then he turned around and walked away.

Once they pulled away Mr. Reeves turned to me. "Do you know how to read?"

My throat felt dry. I hadn't known my father was going to leave me here with him. "No, suh."

"Well, we'll start there."

***

My first lessons were to learn the alphabet and the sounds that the letters make. There were rules: Ain't no other slaves supposed to know to read except me. If I taught anyone, I'd be asking for trouble, Mr. Reeves said.

"Do you want to know why?"

I nodded.

"Why didn't you ask why?"

"My ma and pa told me that Master Marshall doesn't like a lot of questions being asked."

He raised his eyebrows and then folded his arms. "I see. Well, I love it when you ask questions. It lets me know what's going on in your mind. Whatever you cannot ask Master Marshall, you can go ahead and ask me. Understood?"

I nodded excitedly.

"The reason you can't teach everyone else how to read is because not everyone needs to know some things, Azariah. You get to learn how to read because you're special."

I don't know if I had ever felt special. The prospect of this filled me with hope. "What makes me special?"

Mr. Reeves gave a small smile. "Come with me," he said as he made his way inside the church, a white wooden edifice filled with cherry wood and dark furnishings on the inside. He walked down the aisle of the church all the way to the altar, a simple humble area before the large looming pulpit. I followed him all the way.

He motioned for me to have a seat on the pew, and I sat slowly, my eyes wanting to watch him, but knowing I had to keep my eyes down. He came and stood over me.

"Hold out your arm."

I did as he said.

He held out his right next to mine.

"What do you see Azariah?"

What did I see? What was I supposed to see? He was wearing his fine, dark, fancy clothes and I had on my worn, faded beige shirt that was probably once white, and old brown pants. The only thing we had in common was our arms.

"Your arm, sir."

He chuckled and sat next to me. "Something happened when you were born, Azariah. You are lighter than your mother, your father, and most of the rest of the slaves on your plantation. I think God created you as a joke of sorts. A slave boy who looks like a white man."

"But I'm not a white man."

"You're absolutely right," he said, poking my chest playfully. "Never forget that Azariah." He reached for a Bible on the pew and began to open it. "Right here in Genesis 9, it reminds everyone here that your people come from Canaan and that your people were cursed to be servants of us. You all were punished for the evils of your forefathers, and it seems you all still have not learned much since that time, which is why we must remind you so often."

"Master Marshall says he whips us to remind us, right?"

"That's right."

"But you don't?"

He paused and thought to himself before he answered. "My slaves don't stir up trouble like Marshall's slaves."

"How come?"

"I do my work as a parson to teach my slaves what is right. I teach them just what I told you. That this is their place in life, and it won't do them much good trying to change what God has made so. They are provided for, if they do their best: they work, follow directions, then what more could I ask for? So Azariah, I don't need to whip them. They understand that this is how God wanted it."

This made sense in my young mind, and I beamed with excitement. If I could get everyone to believe this, I could help everyone to avoid whippings. "Do you think if I told everyone that back at Master Marshall's plantation and if they believed, then Master Marshall or the overseers wouldn't need to use the whip anymore?"

He smiled. "You see. There you go. That's what makes you so smart and special. Marshall was right after all. You are the right person."

***

"Z-U-R-I, Mama, that's how you spell your name," holding up a paper I had been given by Mr. Reeves to write out Ephesians 6:5. Instead, I was using my time learning how to write everyone's name that I knew. We had no table like they did at the church, so I sat on the floor and tried to keep my letters straight even though the grooves in the wood always messed me up. I had been working with Mr. Reeves for a month now and had learned the whole alphabet and how to spell my name. Every day, I had to memorize a new verse from the Bible. My favorite verse that Mr. Reeves taught me was where Jesus says, "You are my friends if you do what I command you." I liked the thought of Jesus as my friend.

Mama snatched the paper from me, tearing it to shreds, her eyes wild with fear and anger, her fair skin turning red against her simple blue house dress. "Don't you ever tell me that again!"

she said, breathing heavily.

"I...I just thought you'd want to know how to spell it in case-"

"In case of what? In case the Master ask me to write it someday right before he whips me to death?" Still clinging to the shreds in her hands, she looked at me contritely. "Baby, Master Marshall and Master Reeves chose you to learn how to read, not me, not Pa, not anyone else. I know how much you like to help. But, teaching me ain't gon' help me. It'll get me in a lot of trouble and get you in trouble too. Do you understand?"

I nodded.

"I think maybe you shouldn't write here. Maybe only when you're with Master Reeves or Master Marshall,"

"But mama-"

"But mama nothing, remember that verse you told me, children obey your parents? This would be a mighty good time to be obedient."

"Yes, mama."

"Now, go on." I did as she said and left.

But I turned back to look at her through the window and noticed that she was piecing back together the shreds of that paper and taking one last final look at Z-U-R-I, before she dumped those pieces of paper in the water bucket.

***

Learning the correct sounds each letter made took time and practice. Sometimes an E could sound one way and then completely different another time. Reading words felt like counting when I first started. I felt bad that I read slowly and not as freely as Mr. Reeves, his words sounding like a melody. I wished I could make my words flow together the way Mama or Pa sounded when they sang. Or the way the rest of the slaves sounded on the plantation when they snuck off in the night to have church. We used to meet in hush harbors, listening to an old slave man named Lionel. I remember going once when I was small. I don't remember much about what was said. We had no bibles; everything we knew from the Bible was memorized and passed down. In these hush harbors, there was the distinct sound of hope; voices singing in harmony the songs of freedom, Lionel preaching with fervor, even though he had to whisper. When Master Marshall found out about Lionel's preaching to us, he was beaten so badly that he didn't survive. Master Marshall said that by law it was forbidden for any slaves to meet at night, not even for church. We could be meeting to plot against him. When Lionel died, the community that had been built still held up. We could sense it when it someone raised a song of comfort in honor of the one who had just been beaten or sold away.

Mr. Reeves said that when I finished learning and grew older that I would teach everyone the Bible and that they would be able to meet for church during the day. I was excited about that. I would be the answers to both Master Marshall's and the slaves' prayers.

I was such a dedicated pupil, my young mind didn't understand it in this way, but now, I understand that I felt like my life finally had purpose. I would often walk from place-to-place daydreaming about how God would use me. One of those days, I was walking, picturing myself preaching with the same intensity as Lionel. This time I wouldn't have to be quiet in the middle of the woods. This time, I would be at the pulpit, loudly proclaiming the word of the Lord.

"So how have you been enjoying your lessons with Mr. Reeves?" Master Marshall asked me, interrupting my thoughts. I jumped with surprise and fear. Master Marshall rarely spoke to me directly. Did he know that I had tried to teach my mama how to read? Was he angry about that? I had been working with Mr. Reeves now for six months and could read simple books and write simple notes.

"It's been good, suh," I said. Pa always told me to keep my words few with Master Marshall. Only answer exactly what he asked you, no more, no less.

Stroking his chin, he asked, "What's he

been teaching you?"

That was a loaded question, I thought. He's been teaching me a whole lot. Should I tell him about grammar rules? Tell him about how Mr. Reeves says I'm special, but not more special than white people? Or should I quote a scripture for him?

Which would he want to hear? Which response would impress him the most? Even at the tender age of eleven, I knew what he would want to hear. I told him, "That salvation comes from obedience. Obedience to our masters as unto the Lord."

I was right. He smiled wide with approval. "That Reeves is something else. I thought that perhaps he was a fool. He said it worked well in the West Indies, but I didn't believe it. Now, I see there is a method to his madness. There is a method to his madness."

I kept my head down, my eyes low, looking at my feet planted on the ground. "I'm happy to see that you are learning the right things, Azariah. When you get a bit older, I'm sure you'll do well teaching this to others. I may even allow you to teach the other children soon, if Mr. Reeves thinks you're ready. Would you like that?"

I looked up directly into Master Marshall's face for the first time in my life. I was so happy I forgot everything my Pa had told me about that. "Yes, suh! I promise to teach them everything that Mr. Reeves said! I promise I'll make sure that you're proud that they know the Word and their place."

Again, Master Marshall nodded at me and smiled. "Well, you go on and head on to your parents."

***

For two years, Mr. Reeves continued my studies in reading and in the Word. I shadowed him as he preached to his congregation. Well, not really. I had to listen from the outside, I could never set foot inside the door of a white church without risking stripes on my back or possibly my life. I listened to the way that he structured his sermons, the tone that he used, the books from the Bible that he chose to teach. White church was a lot quieter than the hush harbor. Even though we had to be quiet in those woods, we still whispered along amens and our approval at the Word. Here, everyone just sat and listened quietly. Many sometimes even looked bored. Mr. Reeves barely even sweat when he preached. If he did, it was only if it was summer. Mr. Reeves preached mostly on obedience and on the dangers of hell for sexual sin and drunkenness. He also preached a lot on how God had blessed them with their wealth and with their property and how important it was for them to steward their property well. Originally, I thought their property was just their home or their horses, but I realized that he was talking about me.

He didn't automatically turn over the reins to me to be able to preach. First, he let me teach a few of the children, under his supervision, and then teenagers, under his supervision. By the time I was 13, not only was I reading, but Mr. Reeves had fully come to trust me as his protégé. He often left me in his study without checking in on me for increasingly longer periods of time. He advocated for Master Marshall to let me travel to other nearby plantations to teach slaves there as well. I had never been off the plantation before then. As a young man, I finally saw the world outside of Red Oaks, and the places nearby weren't much different than our plantation. White men still traveled to and fro with their slaves in tow. Slaves still had to hold their eyes down when spoken to. I used to think that maybe inside town would be different. One would have to go very far to find a place where you could be free.

When teaching to the neighboring plantations, I taught them everything that Master Reeves had given me, which I now know was only about ten percent of the Old Testament and just small excerpts from the New Testament. When I had asked why Mr. Reeves' Bible looked much bigger than the portions that he allowed me to read, he said, "You are special, Azariah, but not that special."

Once, in passing, I heard Mr. Reeves tell Master Marshall that the Old Testament would inspire too many dreams of freedom, and that Paul reminded slaves that their freedom would only be found in Christ. I didn't know what that meant at the time. All I knew was that I desperately wanted to please Mr. Reeves and Master Marshall and that I was eager to teach and share with the children and teenagers. First, it began on Master Marshall's plantation. I was given a room full of about 50 children ranging in ages 3-16. Some of them were older than me, and the eldest children oversaw keeping the young ones quiet and contained. I taught them a few songs. Not the songs that you would normally hear on the plantation. Those songs were filled with rich tones of deep joy or deep anguish, but instead songs that Mr. Reeves had taught me, like "Just As I Am".

I remember he told me, "When you teach them this song, Azariah, you want to focus on this verse," he said, pointing to it in the hymnal. "Sing it twice if you have to."

> *Just as I am, and waiting not*
> *to rid my soul of one dark blot*
> *to thee whose blood can cleanse each spot*
> *O Lamb of God, I come, I come*

And I did. I always remembered to sing that verse twice. Then I taught them that obedience to your masters was the only way to connect with Christ Jesus and that we had to connect with him to be at peace with our Father in heaven. There are many times that I remember the look on the children's faces as I told them that Jesus said, "You are my friends if you do what I command you," and that if we loved him that we would obey his commandments. His commandments were clear, that we should obey our earthly masters: we should never lie, steal, or cheat our masters of a hard day's work. I taught them what Mr. Reeves had taught me, that we were born for this very role in life, for this privilege to build the nation in this way, and that we would have our reward in heaven for it. I remember those that stared at me with blank faces, not quite understanding, or maybe not quite caring, and those who stared at me with disdain. I knew that this was different from what Lionel had taught us, and I knew that Lionel's words had once filled us with hope; but maybe Lionel had been wrong. Not maliciously so, but maybe the reason we had experienced such pain was because we hadn't just accepted our role in the world.

But now I know the truth, and what haunts me are those who came to me with tears and a broken and contrite heart, begging for forgiveness, begging for help to remember all that I had taught them, begging to remember their station in life and to work harder.

There was a sweet young girl on our plantation that we all called Honey, some called her Sugar, because she worked over at the sugar mill, and she was the kindest soul you'd ever meet. Pa told me that Master Marshall named her Honey because when he went to the auction block, he heard her singing sweetly next to her mother. Yet, he still tore her from her mother's arms and brought her to this plantation where he made her work the fields and then come in and sing for him and his family. He made her sing even when she was getting whipped. He said he didn't like no sad-faced woman, not even his slaves. They should be happy knowing that he was a good master that took care of them.

She was my age, quiet and shy, with a nervous personality. She was the only child that was kind to me. The only one that never commented on my skin or my mother. With no family, my mother took her under her wing, trying her best to protect her, although I know she often could not.

We used to play catch or just run around when we were younger. She had those dark brown eyes that twinkled when she smiled. By the time we hit thirteen, she held them down most of the time. There was a rumor that she came from a line of African queens, which wasn't hard to believe, she always looked regal to me. She had even skin, the color of black coffee, and hair that extended down her back when she braided it. She was still the most beautiful woman on the plantation, even when they beat her mercilessly and cut all her hair for scratching one side of Shaw's face when he attacked her. Jacob Shaw was the overseer over at the sugar mill and he used to frequently drag her into a room. I remember how she used to scream.

She came to me after a few of my teachings, asking me to pray with her for repentance. She desperately wanted to please God. She desperately wanted to be obedient to him in all things. I prayed with her that day. From that time on, whenever she got dragged off by Shaw into that shack, I never heard her scream again.

For all her silence, I do think her soul cried out in those moments and haunted me in my sleep.

***

I worked for many years, completely

brainwashed and oblivious to how Mr. Reeves had conditioned me to not just accept, but to appreciate my own enslavement. I understood why his slaves never acted up. I understood why he never had to whip them. They thought of him as I thought of him, as a wise father. They thought of themselves as I thought of myself, as nothing.

Master Marshall and Mr. Reeves were pleased with the progress of the slaves on the Marshall Plantation. They were calmer, they worked harder, there were fewer instances of public whipping. Three years of preaching to them had left me at sixteen feeling satisfied with the work I had done. Even though it had cost me many relationships on the plantation, namely that of my own mother and father. At nights, my father tried to remind me that Mr. Reeves was not my friend and certainly not my father.

"He don't have no good planned for you son. You a tool in his hand, and when he's done with you, you'll end up in the trash."

I did not believe him, why would Mr.

Reeves and Master Marshall invest so much time teaching me if I meant nothing to them? Even though I stayed quiet and never dared to argue back with my father, he could tell that I did not believe him. My mother could tell that their influence on me was being overshadowed by a larger force at work. She prayed at night for me. She didn't even care whether I heard her or not. I was a lost soul to her in desperate need to be saved.

My parents were far more gracious than the rest who saw me as a traitor and one who had forgotten my own place. One who was privileged and could spout the rhetoric that I did simply because I had never known what it was like to feel a whip across my back. My parents knew that I had no choice but to teach what Mr. Reeves and Master Marshall wanted me to, what they struggled with was that I believed every word of it.

Until I learned more words.

One night, it was after the heat of the summer and the cool winds had started to come, my father asked me to talk with him. We made sure not to go anywhere past the mill, far enough away to talk privately, but close enough where we wouldn't be suspected of running away. Honey once told me that she used to hide out here from Shaw, but I didn't see her around when we approached the mill.

My father had never actually asked to talk to me. He always just started talking. He sat at the front of the door of our cabin, his creamy skin surrounded by the shadows. For the first time, I realized that we were the same height and had a similar build, although he still looked stronger than me.

"You're a grown man now, almost 17 years old. Many men start to marry close to your age," he said.

I nodded. "Maybe one of these days Master Marshall will choose a wife for me."

"You choose a wife for yourself, son."

"But-"

"But, nothing. You meet you a girl that you love and you tell Master Marshall that you wanna marry her. Ain't everything should be decided by Master Marshall."

"Well, then, maybe Honey, or Tildy, they're real nice girls."

He stared at me with slight annoyance and cleared his throat. "You want to know why I named you Azariah?"

He looked out at the expanse of the sky that seemed to meet and just kissed the puffs of cotton. "My mother was like you, Azariah; she wanted to please her master so bad that she lost sight of who she was. He took advantage of her in every way. He did to her what the overseers do to Honey. That's how I was born. I know that I was his child, because the man I knew as my father was as dark as molasses. He still raised me as his own, even when people would say things. He still always told me I was his. He was a preacher like you. He had a kind master as a child, one that allowed him to learn to read, one that let him read the whole Bible. He loved to tell me the stories about the people in Israel being free from slavery in Egypt, and about

Daniel and how he didn't follow the law that told him he couldn't pray, and so they threw him in a prison with lions, and you know what? God protected him. My favorite story was this one about three Hebrews boys, Shadrach, Meshach and Abednego, those were the names they were forced to have, but their real names were Hananiah, Mishael, and Azariah. These boys were told to bow before a golden statue, a false god, and they refused. The evil king had them thrown into a fire. But God was with them, and they didn't burn, they didn't even smell like smoke."

"I've never heard that story. That's not in the Bible."

"That's not in the Bible they give you, son. Because they want to keep the truth from you. That there ain't nothing wrong with you. That all of this is evil. They want you to bow before that god of slavery. But that ain't the true God."

"God wants us to be obedient."

"Yes! But, God wants us to be free!" he said, grabbing my shirt. "Body, spirit and soul."

"Pa…"

"Listen to me! I done stood by for six years and let them fill your head with lies, and I'm gonna have to answer for that someday, because I was too much of a coward to tell you the truth. You gotta find it for yourself son, 'cause you can't keep leading these people astray. It ain't right."

"What do you want me to teach them then?"

I could've sworn I heard him tremble. "Tell them that he loves them. Maybe if they know that, maybe they'll learn to love themselves too."

I furrowed my brow with confusion. I had never thought much about whether Jesus loved me. Only whether my master did. I only thought of how I could prove to Jesus that I loved him, and that was through obeying my master.

"What if they don't let me teach them that? Pa, I could get whipped for that." I thought of how my father's back looked, with zig zagged raised scars across them.

"I told you that you were meant to be a prophet. You ain't Mr. Marshall's prophet, you God's prophet. You say whatever he tells you to and to whoever he tells you to."

He stood up. "You're not special because you look like them. You hear me? You're special because God called you."

He grabbed my arm and held it up. "This ain't nothing but a shell, we leave it with us when we're gone. You wanna hear 'well done, good and faithful servant' someday? Well, do something with that reading and with your voice. Tell the truth. Even if you gotta find some way off this plantation to do it. Lord knows that I tried and that's what landed me in this mess."

"You did? You can read?"

"Yes, that's what got me sold over here, and I promised myself that I would keep you and your ma safe, by keeping it to myself, but it's eatin' me up watching you do this."

To tell the truth on this plantation would be asking for death. The only way would be to run away. "I would never get away from here.

When Kenny did that, they had him ripped apart by the dogs," I said. That had been the most horrific day of my life, the moment I saw them dragging Kenny back onto the plantation. I think he had expected a whipping and most of us did too. But they had unleashed their dogs on him, and forbade any of us to move from our spots as we watched him scream in pain and terror. His family was there, his friends were there, and we all had to just stand and watch.

Pa nodded. "You'll find a way, son. I know you will. When you do, you use what you have to tell everyone about this evil. Who knows, you might even change someone like Master Marshall's mind."

"I'll never be able to change their mind."

"Ain't nothing impossible with God."

***

A week later, I held my mother as she wailed into my arms. They carted my father off in exchange for two teenage male workers. None of us understood why my father had been sold off. He was a good worker that never behaved disloyally towards Master Marshall. The day after my father was sold, I returned to my parsonage duties at the church with Mr. Reeves. I felt as though my head was in a fog of confusion, anger, and sadness. I kept dropping things and forgetting what I was doing.

As I worked on cleaning the church, Mr. Reeves commented, "I heard about what happened with your father. I do feel badly for your father being sold, Azariah. I hope you will find a father in your heavenly Father."

I kept scrubbing at the windows, trying to keep my tears at bay. "Do you know why Master Marshall sold my father?"

Mr. Reeves looked at me and I could tell that he was deciding whether to be honest with me. "Master Marshall believed that your father would be too much of a bad influence on you."

I paused scrubbing. "I don't understand."

"Your father was a troublemaker before."

"But he didn't cause any trouble here."

"Mr. Marshall doesn't believe that people can be changed. He felt that as you grew older that under your father's thumb that he might rub off on you. He became aware that your father had been teaching you falsehoods."

"Falsehoods?"

"Lies about the Word of God."

Someone must've been listening in on our conversation. I wondered who. I needed to know who. But finding out who would not change the transaction. "So, he was sold because of me."

"He was sold to save you. To keep you focused. It will hurt for a while, but the Word reminds us that we must be willing to give up mother and father for the Kingdom."

"Did Jesus say that?"

Mr. Reeves paused. He was used to me asking him questions. He wasn't used to me questioning him. "Yes, yes, he did."

I nodded. I knew what I had to do, and I knew what I had to say. "Well then, I must be obedient. Thank you, Mr. Reeves." He came over and put his hand on my shoulder. "Give your burden to the Lord. He will take it." I thought of my mother who had to reserve all her tears for the nighttime as she crawled into bed alone. All day she worked in their house and had to smile and be at the beck and call of those who only took from her.

I nodded. "He will make it all clear."

"Indeed." I said and continued scrubbing.

Mr. Reeves, "You were given to me by the Lord, and stewarding over your wellbeing is a responsibility that I do not take lightly."

"Thank you, Mr. Reeves." I was his property that he had to steward. He nodded and walked out of his study. As I scrubbed the window, the light from outside poured onto his bookshelf. There were so many Bibles and commentaries. I stared at them and then looked down at the wooden chair where my Bible laid. The spines of Mr. Reeves' bibles must've been at least two inches thicker than mine. What information did he have that I did not know? Maybe if I read it all, then I would understand why God had done this. I noticed as I moved closer to the shelf that Mr. Reeves even had two of the same bible. His favorites always remained close by on his desk. If I could read this fast enough, he wouldn't notice that it was gone.

That day I stole my first copy of the Bible. The whole Bible.

***

In Genesis, I learned that I wasn't a mistake, that I wasn't some cursed individual for the sins of Ham. I was a son of Adam like we all are. Prone to sin. Created by the hand of God. Our sin brought in every form of evil, even the evil of slavery, yet God heard his people in their bondage and sent his servant Moses to aid in their freedom. God wanted them to return to him, but his people had become so comfortable in the place of their enslavement that they still wanted Egypt, their gods, and their way of life. He gave us laws to govern ourselves, but the laws only showed us that we had no capacity to keep them. He continued to be merciful to the nation of Israel despite their sin and grew the nation, numbered them, loved them. He challenged them to come out of the wilderness and to possess the land he had promised their father Abraham. They obtained it but repeatedly forgot who the Lord was and what he had done for them as the generations went on.

Hiding that Bible in our cabin, each night I read on and on about kings and prophets and people who obeyed and disobeyed, and how God loved them and punished them at times, about evil kingdoms that rose and enslaved the people of Israel and how God spoke to them and reminded them to repent. I found out where my name came from, my mother's, my father's, and many other people on the plantation who weren't allowed to even read and learn who they were named after.

Then I learned about Jesus.

He wasn't the man that Mr. Reeves talked about, wholly concerned about my obedience to my master. But he was a complex man. A man that looked nothing like Mr. Marshall, a man who lived with wealth, who ruled as king and ruled with a whip in his iron fist. Jesus lived humbly. Jesus asked hard questions. Moses told them not to murder, but Jesus challenged that if they hated, they might as well have murdered. How did Mr. Reeves and Master Marshall skip over that? Jesus was a man who did miracles. A man that extended grace to people who didn't seem like they deserved it. A man that died a cruel death he did not deserve, for people who did not deserve his sacrifice.

He was not the man Mr. Reeves had taught me about. Jesus is God. As Paul wrote, he is the image of the invisible God of the Old Testament. Mr. Reeves had taught me about a man-made god. One who had been shaped and formed in their own fashion, one with whom they could justify their evils, revel in it and pass it on to the next generation.

I helped them. It was done unknowingly and yet; it was simultaneously unacceptable.

I felt sick. I felt dizzy. The more I read, the

more infatuated I became with understanding who God was: merciful, good, loving, just, holy. I became doubly infatuated with understanding that the institution of slavery was the antithesis of this. There were scriptures that made me unsure how anyone could just omit them.

Exodus 21:16- And he that stealeth a man, and selleth him, or if he be found in his hand, he shall surely be put to death.

Colossians 4:1- Masters, give unto your servants that which is just and equal; knowing that ye also have a Master in heaven.

Maybe Mr. Reeves and Master Marshall did not know. Maybe they had not read this book the way I had. Maybe it was my calling to tell them. I couldn't reveal to them that I had finally read the Bible from cover to cover. I returned the Bible to its place where I had taken it from. Mr. Reeves hadn't even noticed that this copy had been gone for nearly a month. I prayed for days asking God to guide me. How could I share with Mr. Reeves?

On Mondays, I usually swept and scrubbed the floors. I replaced all the books and hymnals in their rightful place. Mr. Reeves spent time in his office, critiquing himself and praying about how he could fix his message. As I cleaned, I approached him carefully.

"Mr. Reeves, how did your service yesterday go?"

"Quite well, Azariah, thank you for asking. How did yours go?"

"Quite well, sir. Thank you."

"What did you teach them?"

"I taught them Hebrews 13:17 sir. Obey them that have the rule over you and submit yourselves: for they watch for your souls, as they that must give account, that they may do it with joy, and not with grief: for that is unprofitable for you."

Mr. Reeves smiled and removed his spectacles, "That is wonderful! I'm sure the workers received excellent teaching."

"Thank you, sir. What did you teach yesterday?"

He put back on his spectacles. "I taught on the perils of the love of money. Nothing for you to trouble yourself with."

I smiled and nodded, just as he would want me to.

But it was then that I realized that Mr. Reeves *kept* the truth from me. Which means he knew it. He knew that the love of money is what fueled slavery, every slave had their price, every slave had to pick a certain amount to keep their master's unearned revenue up. I had assumed the best intentions in the inclusion of Joseph's story and the exclusion of Moses'. I had been told that Joseph had done well to submit to his slavery, and he was rewarded for it. The missing verse about our unity in Christ in Ephesians 3:28 had been intentional. They had made sure not to exclude Ephesians 6:5.

Anger boiled within me. I felt my body grow hot, my palms sweat, and my nostrils flare. My head and heart were drowning in the depths of betrayal. The words burst out of me. "Which while some coveted after, they have erred from the faith and pierced themselves through with many sorrows."

Master Marshall once told Mr. Reeves the day would come that he would realize that mere Bible verses were not enough to keep us in line. They needed force, they needed reminders, they needed a rod, they needed a whip. Master Marshall had questioned whether to kill me altogether. They debated this as they had me tied to the post, waiting for my punishment. I was on my knees in front of the post, my hands trembled and clung to the wood in fear.

"Reeves, he is better off dead. I can't have none of the other trash round here thinking that they can forget their place."

"I understand your sentiments, but he will be worth more to you alive than dead."

"I don't care nothing about money if I lose my respect on my land!" Marshall erupted.

Reeves moved closer to Marshall; I think in an effort for no one to hear. "We will deal with him severely if you insist. But he is a tool, an instrument. Once everything is complete, you will have obedience from everyone here, not just Azariah."

Marshall glared at him, taking even breaths. He then handed Reeves the whip. "Then you whip him. Make it memorable," he said as he started to summon the entire plantation to watch.

We could all tell that Reeves had never done this before. He began to sweat and clutched the whip clumsily. His first swing, he missed me.

"Reeves, if you miss again, I may consider taking the whip to you!" Marshall yelled. Reeves made sure not to miss again.

I had never been whipped in all my 17 years and the pain was sharp and unimaginable, but not as sharp as the pain of watching everyone on the plantation, including the children watch me, their faces filled with fear as they turned their faces inward to their mother's dresses for comfort. I could hear the pain of my mother's whimpers; she dared not cry too loudly and upset Master Marshall. Mr. Reeves gasped to catch his breath after the whipping. Six lashes on my front and ten on my back in honor of the scripture I had recited.

When it was done, Marshall sneered at Reeves. "You are cutting into my money. First, you had me sell his father and now my property is damaged. How could you not suspect that this would happen?"

***

From that day on, I no longer believed in the benevolent slave master. How could there be benevolence when the "subservient" needed to be forced or controlled? But I could not wake up tomorrow and tell Mr. Reeves or Master Marshall that I no longer wanted to be their preacher, that I wanted to teach something different, that I no longer wanted to do their bidding. How could there be a benevolent master when slaves had to be brainwashed to believe that we were meant to be subservient? I was caught between two evils: do I risk my own life and the lives of the others on the plantation by teaching them the truth of God's word? Or do I parrot the muddled truth, no, the defiled lies. They wanted me to teach, to preach, to erode the fabric of human dignity of everyone that worked against their will.

As I lay recovering on a wooden slab, covered with rough sheets used to attempt to make my suffering more tolerable, my mother and other woman applied salve to my wounds, my soul felt whipped and tattered more than my body. James says that "the wrath of man worketh not the righteousness of God". I was angry about the injustices of slavery. I was angry Honey thought that she had to submit to rape, that children had to watch others get beaten and violated on a regular basis, that children themselves were subject as well. I was angry that they felt that perhaps they deserved it. I was angry because slaves walked around hating the skin they inhabited and hated the skin I had too. They hated skin. Too dark and it was ridiculed, vilified. Too light, and it was subject to envy or even another degree of self-hatred to bear the same resemblance to those that committed atrocities against you. I was angry my mother would never know how to read or spell her own name. Later, I learned neither my mother, nor I would ever know our original surnames.

As much as I knew that slavery was not the will of God, that anger began to live, breathe and take up residence within me, until it gave birth to hatred. It was then that I began to plan. I had to leave. The prospects of either of the two evils of risking the lives of others by teaching them the truth or continuing to lie to them wasn't anything I could live with. If I escaped, I reasoned, I would only be risking my own life. I wouldn't tell a soul, not even my own mother. If I told her, she would remind me of what happens when you escape. The fear of what could happen already made my heartbeat so loud I could hear it in my ears, I would shake sometimes, lose my breath, and lose precious moments of sleep. Reminders from my mother or anyone else wouldn't be helpful.

Help came when I was told to drive the buggy and accompany Mr. Reeves to the train station to go preaching down in New Orleans. I was to be his servant on this trip. He and I barely talked the whole way in the buggy. I think he didn't really know what to say to me, and I didn't have anything to say to him besides what was necessary to get us there. It was an annoyance when I was asked to transport him to the train station. But God works in mysterious ways, because when we got to the front of the line to pay for our train fare, I read on that board how much it cost to get to several places in this here United States. Including that it would only cost me $10 to reach Philadelphia. Freedom.

That's when the plan began to unfold. For a year, all I took was small coins from anyone I interacted with. It could be as much as a quarter and as little as a penny. I knew that during certain times of the year, when Mrs. Marshall was planning a large party, or preparing for Christmas; she was careful about her money, so I couldn't take more than a penny. But other times, she wouldn't even notice that a whole quarter had gone missing. I couldn't put two in my pockets because they'd jingle, so, every day, I swiped just a little from Mr. Reeves, Master Marshall, homes I was sent to visit, stores, wherever. I kept them in a box I hid under a broken floorboard and some in the chimney in our little cabin. I wrapped each coin in the torn remains of one my father's old shirts to reduce the jingle of the coins if I needed to grab the box and run. Each day when I came back and wrapped a coin before my mother returned home after the Marshall's supper, I remembered the last conversation I had with him. Every day, I vowed to make it off this plantation.

Caution was important. For the first three months after my whipping, Mr. Reeves, Master Marshall, and the overseers watched me even more carefully than before. I had to earn their trust by convincing them that I was a reformed man in whom the whip had truly initiated repentance. They now began to sit in on some of the slaves' church services. I preached everything they told me to, without deviation. I drove fear and submission into the hearts of the slaves and at night prayed fervently for the opposite.

It was a strange experience living a double life. The Bible says that "a double minded man is unstable in all his ways". It was true, my mind was anxious, divided, choked out by anger and panic at night. But when I rose each morning, I woke up focused on getting more coins.

It had been six months after my father had been sold when Honey approached me one evening as I walked back home after completing my duties to clean Mr. Reeves church.

"Hi, Azariah. How was your day?" she said walking in stride with me. Her voice sounded shaky, like she was nervous to talk to me.

"It was just fine. How was yours?"

She looked down at her feet and nodded her head while saying, "It was fine."

"Whatchu doin' out here? If they see you over here, you'll get in trouble."

"I know," she said quietly. "But I wanted to confess."

I stopped walking. "Confess what?"

She fumbled with her hands. "It's been bothering me so bad. I can't sleep at night. I thought I was doing the right thing, but I sinned. I think I'm going to hell."

My body stilled and I turned to her stiffly. "What did you do, Honey?"

She started crying and blubbering through her words. "Your pa got sold because of me. I heard you and him talking by the mill. I was hiding from Shaw out there. You didn't see me."

"I looked, and it was clear!"

"I was inside under the open window," she said. "When you left, Shaw found me, and I told him, so he'd leave me alone for an extra day. He hurts me real bad, Azariah. I try to be a good servant. I try to be silent, but I don't know if I can do it anymore. I don't know if I can keep letting him do this. He makes me bleed. If I end up with his child, I swear I'll kill myself."

I wanted to rage, but not at Honey. I didn't know who to rage at. Should it be the overseer? He's employed by Master Marshall. Should it be

Mr. Reeves? I'm the one that preached this nonsense to Honey. I held her shoulders firmly. "Listen to me, you not gon' hurt yourself. You hear me?"

Her breathing started to even out.

"I'm not mad at you. I need your forgiveness. I should've never told you to be quiet when that man violates you. It's not right. Hardly anything that I ever teach y'all is right. It's what they want me to teach y'all."

We stared at each other for a bit. Both of us were ashamed. Both of us broken.

She spoke first. "What's the right thing to teach us?"

It had been a long while since I'd truly thought about this. I had been going through the motions of planning my way out of this place that I hadn't done much thinking about this.

"I want to teach you about God's salvation, about his love, and his grace. I want to tell you all that you matter to God, not just because of the work that you do. I want to tell you that what Master Marshall, Mr. Reeves and the overseers do is evil."

She looked confused. "What's grace?"

I smiled. "I'll tell you some other time, a time where you won't get in trouble. Hurry back. I don't want anyone to see you missing from your work."

"Ain't no sewin' or cleanin' need to be done right now. Only waitin' around for Shaw to find me."

"What do you reckon you'll do the next time he finds you?"

She finally looked up at me and a light, a fire flickered in her eyes. "Scream."

***

At night, Honey would come and visit my mother's cabin, and I'd teach them both the Bible in secret. I had memorized many of the scriptures and at least knew the storyline of the Bible. I trusted that neither would say anything to anyone about our secret meetings. We'd talk in the darkness, so that we could avoid too much suspicion. There was a notable change in Honey. The more I taught her, the more she wanted to learn. I realized the fears of slave owners all over Tennessee and the country, because the more she learned, the more she desired freedom. My mother wanted it as well, but she had convinced herself that she was too old for dreams and fantasies. Honey and my mother would often talk about their experiences here on the plantation. It was then that I developed more compassion for the woman's plight.

I had no idea that my mother had also been raped and attacked before. She never explained who was responsible for the violence against her or what happened to her. She wanted to spare me, and I understood her apprehension. I think full knowledge would've cut me too deep at that age. I did not understand the depths of the pain of helping to raise another woman's children, to nurse a white child, to smile and sing to them, to expend all your energy on them, and have almost none for your own children, and only to have that white child turn around and treat you, not as a loving pseudo-mother or grandmother, but as a slave. They knew that their masters viewed them as breeders, as female factories to make them more money. They lived in fear of having a girl child, if she was too pretty, she could be subject to rape. If she was not, then what would that do to her personal outlook of herself?

Those were just the fears for her daughters. Her sons brought another set of unique fears and for both son and daughter, the strong potential of having them sold away from her, or her being sold away from them. Mama felt that she constantly had to behave to avoid too much attention and too much potential harm. I never thought about how she spent her days worrying about how her actions might cause me undue harm from Master Marshall.

Honey became a reason to come home every day, and I was anxious for someone to talk to. She was a soothing, healing balm I had not realized I desperately needed. I began to dream about what it would be like for us to escape this place: me, Mama, and Honey. What would it look like for us to wake up to the sunrise without having to cook a meal for a master, to think about your quota of cotton for the day, to not have to think about how to preach in a way that would please Mr. Reeves, but instead simply just please the Lord?

For Honey and Mama, what would it feel like to live your days without the constant fear for the violation of your body? To live without the threat of violence, to not hear the snap of a whip against flesh and the cries that came next?

I wanted this more than anything but running away alone was already an almost impossible feat. But three people? Surely, it was impossible.

About two months into these secret meetings, Mama became aware that Honey was pregnant. When I finished my duties at church one day, I came home and found Mama and Honey there earlier than usual. Honey was vomiting into a pail and Mama rubbed her back soothingly.

Mama turned and looked over at me.

"She's with child," she said to me solemnly. "Master Marshall said it's fine for Honey to stay with us now."

Honey was distraught. Her eyes held a complete emptiness to them, and she often had to be compelled to eat. As the midwife of the plantation, she had asked Master Marshall for permission to take Honey under her wing, out of concern that Honey may harm herself and the child. Master Marshall gave his permission so long as Mama made sure that the baby came out alive.

Master Marshall came knocking one night. Mama and I opened the door.

"I don't want to waste no time," he said. "Azariah, you've been spending quite some time with Honey and there's no way to know if the child is yours or someone else's."

"Master Marshall, I respect Honey and honor my Lord. The child is not mine."

"Well, as far as anyone is concerned, the child is yours. You'll marry Honey in a week's time." He knew that the child was Shaw's but he'd rather question the integrity of both Honey and me than Shaw.

The next morning when Honey came to eat breakfast, she sat there staring off into space and not even lifting a fork to her food. Mama gave me a knowing look and then stepped outside to give us some privacy to speak.

"Honey," I said.

She did not respond. She continued staring down at her stomach, a look of hollowed sadness on her face.

"Honey," I said once more, reaching for her hand. "You deserve a safe place, and I would like to give that to you."

"Master Marshall tell you to say that to me?" She asked slowly, finally meeting my eyes.

I didn't want to deceive her. "No," I said. "He told me that we are to marry in a week."

"I have no choice." She said resolutely. "I never have a choice."

Her statement nearly broke my heart. I could not force her to marry me. I could not be another man that forced himself on her.

"You do," I said, wetting my lips. "You can say no. My feelings won't be hurt none. If you choose not to marry me, I will help you escape this place before the end of the week. If you choose to stay, I will do my best to provide that safe place for both you and our child."

Her eyes snapped up to meet mine when I said the words "our child". She nodded and then took up her fork and started to eat. She never gave me a verbal answer. She just showed up one day with flowers Mama had placed in her hair. The only time she gave her consent was when she said her vows. We were both eighteen years old when we married. Young, and although we had very little reason to, we still were filled with a great deal of hope.

I knew that my original plan to leave at the end of the year had to wait until after Honey had her baby. I knew this might have been a part of Marshall's plan all along. Slaves with families typically kept their heads down and followed orders to avoid being whipped, their wives and children from being whipped, or sold away, and married folks with children typically didn't run away.

The more Honey progressed in her pregnancy, the more depressed she seemed to be. Every night, she'd sit down in the cabin or lie down catatonically on the bed as I read scriptures to her. I was not intimate with her during this time. I think that would've fractured her more than she already was. I'd just hug her and pray for her and assure her that I would stay here with her and our child. She'd whisper to herself sometimes. I couldn't make out what she was saying, but I let her talk, because it provided me more comfort than her utter silence.

Then one day Shaw dropped down in the field. Dropped down dead, just like that. We didn't know if it was the heat or his heart. It was a mystery. All we knew was that one minute he was there standing with his whip and the next minute he lay there powerless.

Honey was six months into her pregnancy when she heard. I walked into the cabin and knelt at her bedside.

"Honey," I whispered. Her body was turned away from me and she didn't respond. "Honey, Shaw dropped dead in the field today."

She turned round to face me, and she finally smiled for the first time in months. "Azariah, he heard me. Oh, God heard my prayers."

Her whispers.

"Did you pray for him to die, Honey?"

She shook her head. "No, I prayed he would repent, just like you talked about," she said. "Do you think he did? I asked God that he wouldn't do no mo' evil."

"Either he repented or God took him so that he couldn't do any more evil. I do not know," I said.

I thought at that moment that she was a better student of the Word than I was. I would've never prayed for his repentance. I would've prayed for retribution.

***

After his death, Honey started to get out of bed, she started eating, walking, and working again. She was smiling again and the twinkle in her eye had returned. There were times I observed her lovingly rubbing her stomach and thought that she had finally gained the strength to care for her child that was coming into the world.

With Shaw gone, a wall between us tumbled down. One obstacle to her freedom was gone. She was finally free to be herself, at least with me. We began to talk incessantly to each other, as if we were trying to make up for the months of silence. We asked each other anything and everything about one another. Honey seemed like an open book, revealing everything from her fear of critters, to showing me her secret hiding place, and telling me about Shaw. The only questions she hadn't answered were about her family. Honey had been brought here as property from another plantation. She had arrived with no kin.

We could not agree on a name for the

baby, but I had told her that it was her choice. She liked that. When she went into labor, I was not prepared for how nervous I would be. I could hear her groans, and it almost made me want to kick down the door. I wanted to be with her. I wanted to make sure she was safe.

Before that moment, I would've said that Honey and I shared the deepest friendships, yet, in that time behind the door, waiting for her, I realized I loved Honey. The thought of losing her during childbirth seized me with fear. The thought of losing our child filled me with a dread I did not expect.

I could hear Mama encouraging Honey to push and then finally the sound of a newborn cry. When Mama let me in the room, I saw Honey sitting up in bed. She was sweaty and looked tired, and she had never looked more beautiful to me. She was holding a little baby, its skin the color of my own.

"It's a girl," she said, with a wide smile. "I named her Dove."

"Dove," I repeated in a reverential

whisper. "You are so strong Honey," I said, placing a kiss on her forehead as she passed Dove into my arms, allowing me to hold her.

"Francesca," Honey whispered, looking at me.

She saw the question on my face and answered. "My mother was sold from Haiti, and she named me Francesca. Master Marshall changed my name. It wasn't his to change. I'd like to be called the name she gave me."

***

For five years we had as happy a life as we could have. We were captive, but free with each other. Francesca was perhaps the greatest blessing in my life. She was my friend, my love, my life. Some masters forbade marriage, because it made things too difficult when they sold families apart. But I understood why Master Marshall allowed it. Marriage with Francesca made me almost abandon my plans of running away altogether. I kept the money hidden, but for five years it just stayed there, only making an appearance here and there to barter to get more food for my family, or perhaps a small gift for Christmas, something that could stay hidden. Francesca often asked where I had gotten money to get us meat. But I always played coy. I didn't want her to have to lie for me if ever asked. Her ignorance might save her life.

Other than hiding away money and teaching my family the Bible at night, I followed every rule and made sure to protect my family from violence. Both Mr. Reeves and Master Marshall thought that their whipping and not Christ himself was the source of my salvation and transformation.

I'm not sure what had really been taking place in my heart in those five years. Looking back, I think that I had been living in a fractured sense of self. I was deeply fixated on our survival rather than our freedom that I was willing to play the part necessary to hold it together. But at night as Francesca and Dove laid asleep, I would stare at the floorboards and the chimney and seethe with anger that escape was never going to happen. Not safely.

I focused on making sure that Francesca had everything that my words in the past had deprived her of: happiness, safety, a true family. Together we conceived twice and lost twice.

The second time she lost our baby she wept profusely. "I feel like I done failed you. You are my love, and I can't give you any children, but I gave Shaw a child."

I held her. "You never gave Shaw a child. Dove is mine. Through and through." Many men on this plantation raised children that had not been fathered by them. Some walked with those children in their hands, some at their side, and even some at a distance. All of us victims, and every man processed this differently, and the women and children bore the harshest brunt of it.

I was never upset with her. If anything, I couldn't understand the choices that God was making. None of it made any sense to me. Except for Francesca and Dove. Dove was my shadow, the joy of my days. She asked a million questions, gave a million hugs and kisses, and could explain what you needed to make a pie, identify which flowers and berries were safe or poisonous, and memorized a scripture that started with every letter of the alphabet. My Dovie.

Once her color came in, she had skin that reminded me of my father's, the color of raw sugar, and an explosion of curly hair, and eyes that resembled the most serene skies. She could've easily passed for my daughter, but her eyes always made people question things.

My mother talked to Master Marshall and got him to agree to let Dove shadow my mother working in the house. The house made me nervous, but the field filled me with terror for Dove. Honey did not want her out there with her. It was too grueling, and Dove was too playful and inquisitive for the fields and Master Reeves did not think it was women's work to be in the church studying.

My mother felt Dove would be safest with

her. She was right, none of us could ensure her safety, but she had the greatest chance with my mother's close eye on her. My mother and her friend Chloe watched Dove and made sure that she stayed out of trouble, that she learned all the rules of when to speak and more importantly, when not to speak and how to wash dishes and complete household chores for Mistress Marshall and her daughter. I felt comfortable with her staying with Chloe. She was a God-fearing woman, who always maintained the utmost kindness and loyalty to my mother. She and her husband George lived their entire lives by prayer and singing, it was often their voices singing in the hush harbor all those years ago, and sometimes I suspected that they still met there.

Every day, after I finished working with Reeves at the church, I would head over to the house to pick up Dove and take her home for dinner. On our walks home, we'd talk about the Lord. She loved praying to God and often remarked that Chloe had taught her that she could just talk to God like he was a friend nearby. I marveled at how she would pray about anything, the simplest things, and then ever so often, she'd come back and tell me how God had answered her prayer.

As Dove, Francesca, and I sat eating dinner one evening, Dove said, "Daddy, I prayed that Mistress Marshall would be nice and give me candy someday and she did! Can you believe it? She gave it to me and said that I'm growing up to be a nice little house slave and that someday she'll want me to do what Grandma does!" My mother could never join us for supper because she had to ensure that the Marshall's got their food, that everything was clean, and everyone had retired to bed. Once I was done with my work at Mr. Reeves house, I would stop by the big house to pick up Dove and carry her home.

"That ain't something to be proud of, Dovie," I said.

"Azariah," Honey said softly.

"I don't want her comfortable being called a house slave for some candy," I said, my jaw tight.

Honey shot me a look and then turned to Dove. "Daddy is not angry with you Dove. He's angry with Mistress Marshall."

I cleared my throat. "Your mama is right. I am not angry with you. Listen to me," I said, holding Dove's hand. "You are child of God. You are my child. You are loved beyond measure. Never take joy in anyone calling you anything that makes you anything less than that. Do you understand?"

She thought for a moment. "Yes, I think I understand. Maybe I'll pray that Jesus helps Mistress to see who I am. Is that ok?"

I was about to say that prayer would be futile, but Honey took one look at my face and responded before I could. "That would be a good prayer, Dove," she said, with a reassuring smile.

"Daddy, I had a dream last night."

"Mmmm hmm," I said. This was a regular occurrence. She'd tell me about a dream with her getting candy from me or with us being able to run to an open field and watch the clouds and have butterflies land on our noses. "What'd you dream about?"

"I dreamt about Naima."

"Who's Naima?"

She shrugged. "I don't know. But she's coming and I remember that she had Master Marshall's candlestick with her."

I laughed. "You and your imaginary friend need to settle down. You haven't been messing with Master Marshall's candlestick, have you?"

"No, Grandma said I can't touch it, even though she dusts it every day. It's pretty, but I don't see what's so special about a candlestick."

I didn't know anything about Master Marshall's candle stick either. It stayed on his desk; its golden beauty evident to see. It was old, but the weathered gold made it even more beautiful. My mother was the only one that knew about it and once told me. She had been shaken up because she had narrowly escaped a whipping. Master Marshall's son and daughter had been playing in the house and had knocked over the candlestick and my mother had been in the process of putting it back on his desk when Mistress Marshall had walked in. She instantly blamed my mother, and ready for an opportunity to finally get her whipped, brought her before Master Marshall, but not before firmly hitting her across her face, enough to bruise her.

He did not whip her; instead he believed what she said about his kids playing and accidently knocking it over, and he told her the strangest tale. Mama said that Master Marshall, for some reason, liked telling her stuff.

I remember she said to me, "Azariah, he thinks that candlestick has some sort of magic."

I laughed and snorted. "Magic?"

"He says it belonged to his grandfather. He came over from England and didn't have much money, but he said the man he won it from bet more money than he had and could only give him some cash and that golden candlestick. It's pure gold. His grandfather won it from a man from Portugal. The man said that he had it made in Africa, and he thinks that some African shaman must've put a spell on it because every time it burns its 7th candle then the man is ruined. He burned his 7th candle on it and now he was losing that gambling match and his last two slaves."

"That's nonsense," I said. "So why don't he just give away the candlestick?"

She shrugged. "It don't matter what we think. He said the money from the candlestick is his security, his grandfather told him that he just can't burn that 7th candle on it. He said his grandfather said, 'Just keep it on 6 and you'll be rich'. It's what he lives by, he said everyone says their lucky number is 7, but his is 6."

My thoughts floated back to the present as I heard Francesca talking to Dove. "That's right, don't you go touchin' nothin' in that house."

"Yes, mama," Dove said. "But Naima is coming, I remember it from my dream."

I tapped her hand gently. "Tell Naima to stay right where she is. Ain't nobody want to come to Red Oaks."

I remained silent for the rest of the dinner

as Dove and Francesca talked, and then I excused myself so I could work on the next sermon. It was close to Christmas time, and I wanted to know how I could preach the Christmas story without delving into topics that might land me with another beating, losing my eyes, getting quartered, or even hanging from a tree. That night we lay in bed and Francesca said to me, "You remember when I was pregnant with Dove and you said that if I wanted, you'd help me escape?"

I turned to her. "Why you asking?"

She put her hand to my face. "Azariah, I want to be free. I want Dovie to be free," she spoke with desperation in her voice, and it scared me. "One day she's gonna grow up, and she's gonna end up like me and every other woman on this plantation."

I would never let them touch Dove, not for a beating, not for anything. "Over my dead body."

"Yes, he'll kill you and still take Dove," she said. "We have to be free, Azariah. Any children we have will be Master Marshall's, just like he always wanted. Why you think he doesn't stop the overseers from raping us? Why you think he rapes us? Why you think he tells everyone how many kids they have to have? Because all these children become his."

What could I say to her? I didn't know what it felt like to be raped, to be pregnant with a child you never planned for, that you knew would grow up enduring pain, only to be beaten, abused, and owned.

"Where would we go?" I asked.

"North."

I sat up and shook my head. "We're not going to make it. Not a family of three."

"We have to figure it out." She shook her head. "I don't know. We can try to wait until the summer when it's warm, but the winter might be the best. They're not expecting it."

"We'll freeze to death. Do you want Dovie to watch us torn up by dogs, whipped to death, do you want her with a brand burned into her face?"

"I don't know," she said, with equal agitation. "I haven't thought that far. I thought we could plan together. I thought you wanted to leave here," her voice was shaking. There were tears in her eyes.

Did I want to escape this place? Yes. Did I think that we would be able to successfully escape the plantation and make it North with a wife and a five-year-old? No. Did I think it was worth the risk? I wasn't sure.

"No one can love Exodus so much and not dream of running," she said. "I know you have thought of running. Let's all run together. We can be free. We can dance. We can live by the water and watch Dove grow up. I know that's what you want. It's what we both want."

She was right. After knowing the Bible, the full Bible, I had a daily growing desire for freedom. If I did it alone, I felt I could make it, but to do it with a family? I already had spiritual freedom, but I wanted physical freedom as well. I couldn't wait for the Lord to change the minds of my masters. Even if he did, there would be all the other slave owners in the vicinity ready to re-enslave me. The only way it could come was to have courage and to take advantage of the opportunity I had.

She held my hands. "I owe you so much after what I did to your Pa." She pulled something from underneath the bed. They were the fine clothes of Mr. Marshall. "He has a lot more. He won't miss it."

"Fran-!" I said, snatching it from her, hiding it back underneath our bed and looking around to see if anyone had been around.

"Listen to me, Azariah! You got some things the rest of us ain't got. You can read, you can write, you can talk fancy like them, and you got their skin. Let's use it!"

"I can't do this. Do you know how dangerous it will be for all three of us to go?"

She nodded her head. "We have to try. You can pose as a white man and Dove and I could be your slaves that you're traveling with. We can use those coins you hiding under the floorboards," she said with sass.

"How did you-"

"I was looking for somewhere to hide the clothes and found enough money to get us far away. Don't worry, I have some coins of my own too. It might not be as much as yours, but I've got some."

I narrowed my eyes. "It's not going to work. I cannot risk your lives. I will never be able to sleep, I will never be able to live if something happens to you or Dove."

"I know," she said, with a tortured pain, and then she wiped away a tear. "But you won't be able to live with yourself when they take Dove. Azariah, it will happen, and you won't be able to stop it."

I held my head in my hands. "I promised you a safe place."

"I didn't marry you for that promise. I knew you would never be able to keep it. I married you because I loved you."

My head was spinning. I had thought of this for so long, but suddenly the decision seemed like a weight and a burden I was afraid to carry. How could I blend in as a white man, knowing that I was not one? Where would I go to find white abolitionists? I didn't know the outcome of any of this, but one thing I knew was certain was that Francesca was right when she said that it was not a matter of if violence would happen to us, but when violence would happen to us.

In the silence that enveloped our cabin, I felt Francesca's fingers lace themselves with mine and she kissed me tenderly on the cheek. "I know you think that this skin you've been given is a curse. But I think what you've shown me all this time is God don't make mistakes. God is gon' use this skin, this mind, this voice to do some great work. You always tell me to just be available to him, to do what he says, and everything will be alright. Ain't that right?"

I didn't answer her, and she continued her dreams and her planning aloud.

"Your name will be Jesse," she said. "Your new name."

She looked at me with a smile on her face

and my heart stopped racing for a bit. "Where'd you come up with a name like that?" I asked.

"There was a white boy there at the auction. He was maybe twelve or thirteen. Looked like he came with his pa or something. He looked terrified. Like he was downright sick from being there. From seeing all of us having to stand there and pretend to be happy that was getting sold. They made the women take off their clothes and they forced us to show them our teeth. Anyways, he came to us when no one was looking and he gave us some biscuits and he just said, "I'm sorry", like he was trying to say he was sorry for everyone, for everything, sorry for it all. He said his name was Jesse."

Jesse what?"

"Hmmmm... Anderson."

"Jesse Anderson," I said, trying out the name.

"That's all he ever got to say to us, and I never forgot what he said, or the biscuits, or the look on his face."

"He probably grew up and bought some

slaves off the block himself."

She shook her head at me. "No, not him. Not the way he looked at us. If he bought them, then he freed them, I know it."

"I ain't never met a good one, Francesca."

"They out there," she said. "We gon' meet 'em. My mama used to tell me that my name meant free, I remember that. When I leave here, at least my name will be true."

***

For weeks Francesca kept asking me about my plans. I had none to share with her. Every time I thought of a plan, I instantly broke out into a cold sweat. Then Francesca came home one night in February in a flurry of panic.

"Master Marshall is gon' be selling people to pay off debts."

"Debts from what?"

"That man gambles and spends money on whores whenever he can. I heard him talkin'. He's gonna be selling off some of us. The man he's selling to wants me. We have to go."

The moment we had feared had come. "The plan isn't ready."

"It has to be," she said.

"Francesca, I will figure this out. Please be patient."

Her eyes searched mine and she put her hands and both sides of my face and nodded. "I love you," she said. That evening she stayed inside, told me she needed some time alone to pray, and wanted me to stay with Dove.

The next morning when I woke to find her and Dove gone. She didn't even take any of my coins and I didn't understand why she hadn't. But, if I knew Francesca, she was just thinking of what would be best for me instead of what was best for her and Dove. Mama hadn't even known what she was up to, and Chloe told me that she had just asked for some extra food. Chloe assumed that maybe Francesca was pregnant. The food was to carry with them, and her last "I love you" had been her telling me goodbye. Last night was the last time I held my wife and daughter.

Both Ma and I took a beating the night she left. They were convinced we knew where she had gone. The beating did not equate to the emotional pain I felt from knowing I would never see my wife or daughter again. I prayed I didn't. For them to be found and brought back would be worse. For the first time, I was angry with her. I was angry with her for leaving me, for taking Dove, for not giving us a chance to escape together, even though I knew I had never actually planned to escape together.

For days, for weeks, and even months, both Mama and I lived in fear that one day we'd see Francesca and Dove being brought back to the plantation. But they were never found. It was a cause for rejoicing.

Sometimes, I picture her in Philadelphia or New York, I picture her bright smile and her dancing to music. I think of how Dove may look now. Sometimes, I become filled with dread that they may have succumbed to a lack of water or frozen to death. I wake up my clothes wet from night terrors of them being whipped or torn apart. Oftentimes, when I come home to an empty place, no sound of Dove's laughter or soft footsteps, no sound of Francesca's humming, I find my eyes burning, my chest tightening, and tears begin to flow uncontrollably. I miss them terribly. I must have faith in these moments even though I struggle many times to. Regardless of whatever happened to them, I am comforted to know that they are free in both body and spirit.

After Francesca's escape, I could not bear to leave Mama. I was afraid of what would happen to her in my absence. To have two people from the same cabin flee within a year would subject my mother to a great deal of suspicion and to inflict the worst imaginable pain on her. I could not do it. The clothes that Francesca had given me remained carefully hidden. I dug back into my work full force and remained committed to preaching the word of God. Mr. Reeves and Master Marshall both agreed that an overseer or slave driver needed to be present during church meetings. However, I made sure to remain consistent with Mr. Reeves' teachings until the overseer or slave driver thought that it was futile to continue attending. They would slip out of the building at times to do other things. I saw these moments as my opportunity to share the true gospel to the plantation.

Initially, many of my fellow workers had a general distrust of me. They still believed that I was privileged, arrogant and complicit in the master's tactics against the rest of the slaves. There were times I continued to battle with self-loathing. I wished that my skin would've been darker, and I tried to stay out in the sun more, but just like the master, it did not tan my skin, instead, it made me red and burned. I understood why they felt I was complicit; I was the one delivering these false teachings to them. I was the one during the whipping, saying scriptures of obedience. I offered to pick with them at times, I think this did help my rapport with some of the men and women, but it did nothing to change that my lot was different than theirs. Sometimes, I think many of them only respected me because they held great respect and admiration for, and like me, desperately missed my wife and child.

They had been the ones that had labored with them, not me. Francesca had once worked in the house until Shaw had set his intentions on her and convinced Marshall to have her out in the field. Even though Shaw was dead, she still chose to work out there, having built bonds with those there. When she did work in the house, she often snuck out to bring food and water to those who had worked in the field. She was careful and had never been caught. I did not know what it was to be forced into the field to work, but I did know what it felt like to have no choice, to participate in this cyclical spiritual, emotional, and physical brutality. We had been pitted against each other, not to blame the true perpetrators, but to blame one another for things that we had no control of. No matter our different tasks on that plantation, none of us knew freedom. When I wasn't under the careful guise of the master, overseer, or slave driver, I made sure to share with them my true intentions. Over time, and built trust as I shared the gospel, and refused to act as an informant to Master Marshall, some of them began to trust me.

I was grateful that most seemed responsive to the message of the gospel. I realized that the Holy Spirit of God had been at work during those times in the hush harbor. Even though Lionel had no Bible to read or preach from, many understood that God is holy and that we are not. That our sin caused separation between us and God. God in his goodness, created a path for us to be reunited with him. Jesus, the Son, came to earth, lived a perfect life in our place, and then God placed all our sin on him while he was on the cross. He died as a sacrifice for us and then rose from the grave to conquer sin and death once for all. *This* was the gospel. What God had done through people like Lionel, and I suspected Chloe and George, gave these people the foundation of what they needed to know. I had merely provided them with a more defined structure.

What Reeves, Marshall, and all other slave owners had given us, had never been the good news. They had butchered the gospel, taken whole books and passages out and had given us a faulty text that was only meant to support the furtherance of slavery, to insulate themselves from the guilt of their sin, and to persuade us that we were not human, not worthy of the very salvation that Christ had freely given to all. It was a grievous sin against God's creation, and it was a sin that I would never forgive.

I actively made it my duty to make sure that those on my plantation knew the truth, even if it would mean my death. They all kept the secret. None told the master what they had been learning. They began to sing new songs on the fields, and I could hear hope rising from there with each passing week. Hope in a risen savior, hope in his love for us, hope in his presence with us amid our suffering, because he too had been rejected by this world and had suffered.

Though my hope of escape seemed

dashed, I could feel the deep feeling of peace beginning to rise in me. In 1820, a twist of events occurred, and my mother had fallen one day and began to seize on the kitchen floor during her duty. George rushed in, his eyes frenzied, and came and told me. His wife Chloe and my mother both worked in the house and were close friends. By the time I ran over to the house, her seizure had ended, but she lay lifeless on the ground, and I stood frozen looking at my once strong, vibrant mother, a shell of herself. Had I been so preoccupied with my own troubles that I had not noticed how thin she had gotten? That she looked much older than I realized? She never woke from that seizure and died ten days later. My grief was immense. If I thought the cabin was empty before with Francesca and Dove gone, now it just seemed like I was completely alone in the world. My tears had become my food. The thought of escape was dwarfed by this visceral pain that she had died so suddenly and that I had not been paying close enough attention to notice that my mother had needed me after losing my father, Francesca, and Dove.

The Marshalls felt her loss as well. My mother had kept their home clean all my life. The cherry wood and red carpet that Master Marshall loved was dusted and clean. The pink drapes in Mistress Marshall's room that she used to escape from the reality that her husband preferred slave women to her was immaculate. Mama had cooked for them, anything they wanted, helped rear their son and daughter, cared for Mistress Marshall when she was pregnant with her son and daughter. Mistress Marshall had struggled to have children, perhaps because Master Marshall was so busy with slave women, no one knows for sure. Women who worked in the house said that the Lord had closed her womb because she was just as evil, if not more so than Master Marshall. The women in the house secretly mourned when they found out for the first time that she was with child. Their sense of justice seemed to have been dashed.

When she gave birth to her first son in 1812 and then a daughter in 1814, it was a source of jubilation and pride for both Master and Mistress Marshall. Marshall's son, Charles, was so fond of my mother when he was an infant that he thought my mother was his. This often enraged Mistress Marshall, who in turn would find every reason that my mother ought to be whipped. If anything broke in the home or if an area wasn't impeccably cleaned, Mistress Marshall would demand that Master Marshall should beat Mama. Master Marshall often refused, saying that he had no reason to believe that Mama had been responsible for the mishap. So, Mistress Marshall took it upon herself to make sure Mama stayed in her place with regular slaps to the face for non-credible accusations of insubordination. Chloe received similar treatment for taking care of the Marshall's daughter, although Mistress Marshall hated my mother more.

Once Charles got older, he also broke my mother's heart, as the once sweet child whom she would sing songs of praise to, who would touch her face adoringly, now learned from his parents that he could command Mama's attention and refer to his once thought "mother" as a "mammy" instead. The moment she passed, she was no more than a dead slave to them. Mistress Marshall merely mourned because she had no more outlet for her anger against her husband. Little Charles Marshall no longer had someone who made his food just the way he liked it. Master Marshall seemed to take her death the hardest because he had one less good, obedient, and profitable slave.

At first it was a mystery to everyone when Master Marshall assigned a young woman to my mother's position instead of Chloe. Chloe had been born on this plantation and had worked in the house her whole life. Poor Mara, everyone knew that her child, Meadow, that served as the Little Miss Marshall's companion was the product of Master Marshall's immorality. The Marshalls spent all their day critiquing this woman, telling her how Venus used to do things just the way they liked it. I remember that she had suffered greatly. I moved around the cabin and through my duties like a dead man alive. I had no father, no mother, no wife, no daughter. Master Marshall and Mister Reeves had begun to tell me that it was prime time for me to take another wife. They needed me to marry and have more children. Francesca's words came back to me.

Why you think he tells everyone how many kids they have to have? Because all these children become his. It was then that I knew I could no longer stay there. I could not allow him to take anyone or anything else from me.

I hadn't decided when I would run. The next day, I was doing some work for Mr. Reeves as he asked me questions about my upcoming sermon. I told him what he wanted to hear, that I would be focusing this week on obedience. I only had a limited list of acceptable things I could speak on: obedience to God through obedience to your master, gratitude expressed to God through gratitude for your current enslavement, trust in God and one's master, peacefulness, gentleness and meekness to dare not think of coming against your master. This was his gospel. This was not *the* gospel.

"I'm very pleased with the work that you have been doing on the Marshall plantation. The people there appear happy, satisfied, and Master Marshall reports that they have been doing a fine job with their workload."

"Thank you, sir."

"It grieved me to hear about your mother and the runaway girl."

"Thank you for your concern, sir. I am grateful for it."

"It must've cost Master Marshall a great deal to lose two fine workers, and one future worker."

My skin began a slow heat that burned to my head and the tips of my ears.

"A great deal indeed," I responded.

All we ever were to these brutes was the embodiment of money walking around. We were not people to them who hurt, who cried, who loved, who were human. They could not be obedient to God to free us, to see us as their equals, because their desire and love for money had effectively blinded them. They had erred from the faith and my escape would pierce them with sorrow. I would see to it.

***

I knew that this plan would not be easy. It felt hard before I had a family, impossible to do with a family and even though I felt the immense weight of terror, I had to honor Francesca's memory by following her plan. I would use the money I had collected to get a train ticket and get as far North as I possibly could, posing as white man by making sure to fashion my hair properly and wear the clothes Francesca had gotten from Master Marshall's wardrobe. The fact that I spent so much time around Mr. Reeves meant that I could speak in a way that would more closely mirror whites. I could also read. This would help me. Francesca told me to use what I had, and I intended to do so.

So far, I had enough money to buy a train

ticket. But how would I leave without anyone noticing and throw the dogs off my scent before I got to the station? The days before I left, I washed the clothing that Francesca gave me. As I was washing the clothes in what I thought was the secrecy of my cabin, Mara approached me, holding Meadow's hand. She was a pretty little girl, probably just on the cusp of puberty.

"You plannin' on runnin' away." She wasn't asking.

I jumped to my feet and closed the door as calmly as I could, trying to steady my voice. "Who says?"

She looked me straight in the eye, not willing to continue this act. "Can you take Meadow with you?" She didn't plead. She merely just asked, almost emotionless. Mara was a strong, prideful woman, that never let her guard down and I knew that even this request took a great deal of humility for her to ask. She wanted to protect Meadow.

"I'm not sure that I could keep her safe with me." This was my exact worry when

Francesca wanted me to take a whole family with me. What would it look like to take a young girl? I may have to hide. What if nights got cold? How could I feed her?

She nodded and then said, "You could pretend that she's yours. I know you a holy man, so you don't want to lie to nobody. Just tell them the truth and let em' think whatever they want. Tell them your wife died and that you still grievin' and can't live here no more. So, you headin' North to start over."

What she said made sense, but I looked at her skeptically. Traveling with a child was no longer a part of the plan. She pleaded with me, "Please, she looks like you. It could work."

I looked at Meadow standing there uncomfortably, she barely knew me, only heard me on Sunday preaching lies, her skin was as clear as mine and her face filled with apprehension. She did not want to come with me. She did not even understand why her mother wanted her to go with me. "I'll try to come back for her."

Mara straightened, and her soft pleading face went hard, and she scoffed. "If you make it back, then you're as good as dead. That's ok, Azariah. I won't tell nobody, even if you don't take her with you. I'll make sure that Meadow gets to freedom, one way or another."

I nodded.

She moved and picked up my jacket.

"Here let me help you," she said, and she revealed something in her hand. She started to wrap my clothing in vanilla sticks to remove as much of my scent from it. "You'll need to keep the dogs off of your scent for as long as possible." She then handed me a razor and a comb. "When you get on your way, shave your face and clean up. Master Marshall has so many of these things to groom himself, he won't notice that these are gone." It reminded me of what Fran had said to me when she first gave me the clothes and told me of her plan. I wept that night thinking of her, remembering her laugh, her embrace.

"Thank you," I said incredulously. I did

not expect her kindness after refusing to carry Meadow. "Once I know the way there, I'll come back to get Meadow."

She eyed me. "Don't make promises you can't keep. I told you before, I'll get Meadow to freedom, one way or another."

I nodded my understand. "Thank you, Mara," I said squeezing her hand. Then I took out a few of my coins, still wrapped in my father's shredded clothing and gave them to her. "For Meadow. If I don't make it back, take this and get her North."

She took the coins, gave a small smile and softly said "thank you" before she turned and walked back to the big house with Meadow in tow.

***

I had choices: go west, go south, or go north and hopefully hit Illinois. All of them presented great risk because I would have to go a considerable distance through slave territory before eventually landing in free territory. It was fall and the weather wouldn't be too hot or cold. It would do me good to leave at night. Leaving at night was expected. It was the way Fran had left. They had already assigned someone to be on watch at night. No one would expect anyone to run during the day.

That's exactly what I did. On my way home from work one day, bag in hand with what Reeves thought were just my bible notes, and not a full suit of clothes, I dodged into the woods and ran and ran as far as I could. I could hear my heart beating in my ears, and the dried leaves and twigs under my feet as I ran. My skin felt hot against the wind that whipped around me. No one would expect me to run during the day, and no one expected me, Azariah, the preacher, who told them that it was good to be a slave to actually run away. I could imagine the rumors that would be spreading once word spread that I had run. I hoped I had time to create distance between myself and the plantation. I had to avoid all major pathways, because even though my skin was light, my head filled with loose silky curls, anyone who found me would still question where I had come from. I must've run on and off for six hours north in the backwoods before I hit the river. I scrubbed myself in that cold river. I wanted to wash myself clean of every scent that would attach me to the Marshall Plantation. I tried to shave my face in the fashion of the men I had seen, but I failed and ended up shaving my face clean. I was twenty-five years old when I dipped myself under the water as Azariah Marshall and came back up as Jesse Anderson. I donned my new suit and made sure to finger comb my hair and walk into the next town confidently even with a wrinkled shirt and suit.

To this day I'm not sure what caused the shift in me. I don't know how I entered that river with the mindset, gait, and look of a slave, yet left it as not only a free man, but one that had always been privileged with freedom, one that would be known to passersby as a white man. Perhaps it should've been concerning to me how easily I moved into this new way of being. But at the time, I was just grateful for how easy it had been for me, as if maybe it had been a part of me all along.

It was as if I had been reborn somehow, and I hoped that as I walked about that I would not be suspected by anyone. Somehow, I knew that they would not suspect someone with their own skin color to be three-fifths of a person walking among them.

I walked straight up to a man, looked him in the eye and asked him who I could see about getting a ride to Missouri. Mara had been wrong about me not wanting to lie, because it came so easily to me to explain away my unkempt appearance at the misfortune of having gambled away most of my possessions, except this fine suit on my back and the five dollars in my pocket to head up North to visit my relatives. I didn't want to ask for a ride all the way to Illinois. I had to be wise with every move that I made from here on out. I believe that God led me to Mr. Yeaman, a simple man who just seemed delighted that I had offered him five dollars to take me there. He asked if I minded traveling with a few other folks he had been paid to transport. I did not.

I made small talk with Mr. Yeaman in a simple wagon that had a hard wooden bottom for carting hay. We discussed the state of the Union, and I marveled at how easy it was for me to sound just like them. I'd had years of practice with Mr. Reeves. Mr. Reeves seemed to feel more at ease when I talked to him with more formality. Master Marshall demanded that I talk to him as if I could barely string a sentence together. In both circumstances, I had to submit to whatever each of them wanted of me, of how they preferred to relate to me. Yet, with neither could I forget that I was the subordinate, that even though I spoke with Mr. Reeves formally, I had to still dull down my intellect and pretend that he was the "all wise" teacher and I was merely an ignorant student.

"Those Yankees need a wakeup call. They think that ruinin' people's livelihoods is what's gonna save this nation. They'll be the death of us if they get rid of all we've done down here."

I nodded enthusiastically.

"We're helping them out, you know. We make sure they have food and shelter. And all they do is try to laze around anyhow. The North should be thanking us that we have good values down here."

I nodded enthusiastically again.

I found it fascinating that he just assumed that I agreed with him from just a few nods at the right moments. I had convinced him that I was on his side and for a good portion of our trip he continued to gripe to me about the North, and how those tar babies needed to know their place, and that freedom would just make them think that they were better than they were. He did ask me what I would be doing in the North and I told him that I was a preacher. I recited the messages I had been preaching all these years on the plantation. This endeared me to him even more. He had to make a delivery in Illinois, and he asked if I would like to join him.

It was divine providence.

He liked me so much from our conversations that he seemed not to give much thought to a perfect stranger wanting to travel nearly 500 miles from their original destination. We made multiple stops along the way and stopped at houses and he would always introduce me as a friend. Although we stopped in other places along the route in Tennessee and Kentucky, not once did I garner suspicion from a white person. I had only four dollars left, so I used two dollars to buy more clothes along the way and was even offered some by a woman in Kentucky who appeared to be shopping for a new husband.

When I finally left the South and entered Illinois it was a feeling that I often have trouble explaining. The tightness and pounding in my chest now released. I wanted to cry tears of gratitude, of joy, of relief, but I had to keep every emotion contained for fear that those around me would notice something amiss. Illinois still seemed too close to the border of the South, so

I aimed to get to Michigan. I traveled another three hundred miles to Cass County, Michigan.

For the first time I felt like I could be who I was: a black man, with milky white skin, a former slave who had found freedom. This had once only been a dream.

Azariah
CASS COUNTY, MICHIGAN
1825

"Can you tell us one of your stories?" Grace asked.

I turned back around to face a room of six little ones, children who had come to us after being separated from their parents as they navigated the different stations of the railroad. I had become a conductor after seeing the number of freedmen and women pouring into Cass County. They had sacrificed everything to arrive here and were in desperate need. I knew the arduous journey from South to North, but my skin had shielded me from the worst of it. These children had been hiding in the forests and swamps for weeks or months to get here to freedom. Their parents had sacrificed themselves to make sure their children would no longer have to bear the whip, abuse, or shackles again.

I had been working at the church and helping as a conductor for about a year when those of us at the church first came upon a child, around the age of five, roaming the streets without shelter or food, her feet blistered, her body filthy. When she had come to us, the women at the church had given her a bath. I remember dumping out water so dark gray that it almost looked black. She had come up with her mother and father. Her father had been captured along the way, and her mother, right after they had reached Michigan, had passed away. She had frozen to death, curled around her daughter to protect her from the frigid winter.

In the four years I have been here, it has taken me some time to appreciate the physical differences between Tennessee and Michigan. I love the greenery of Michigan during its summers. Autumn is far more beautiful here, but the winters are harsh. However, even though I must deal with frigid winters, they are still spent free from hearing brutality around me. I no longer live in fear of violence or capture. Other free blacks live around me in freedom. We support one another and assist other runaways. When I first arrived here, they helped me to obtain fake manumission papers. I found a church. I was attending for a year before they asked me to preach my first sermon there, and within another four years, I was being asked to pastor this church. We helped so many people find freedom here, physically and spiritually.

I had been there personally when we rescued Grace, who is now nine. We rescued another little girl named Mercy, about a year after Grace came to us. The names seemed to be providentially chosen, and the girls themselves providentially chosen for us and each other. They were the same age and played and referred to each other as sisters. The ladies at the church always mention that they seem to be destined to find each other given how both have skin the color of cinnamon sticks and their hair a puff of massive curls that the ladies are always trying to tame.

In my third year of being a conductor, just shy of one year before I became the pastor, three brothers joined us, Robert, Clarence, Richard. Three rambunctious, but respectful boys. When they joined us, they were ages eight, seven, and five. Their father had left to fight for the Union army, and when their father died in the war, their mother took sick and never recovered. You could easily tell that the boys were all related, they all looked almost like carbon copies of each other, the same dark skin with their wide smiles.

I never remarried, and the older ladies in our congregation often chastised me and told me that while they admired my devotion to Francesca, that there were plenty of women here that were lovely, kind, and in need of husbands. I agreed with them, but Francesca's memory still looms over me. The loss of her and Dove still feels fresh some days. I spend most of my days in the church and go home when it is very late once the ladies and I, who are helping to care for the children, put them to bed for the night. Usually, nights consist of bedtime stories, and it helps to have kids around to heal the loneliness and loss.

"Which story do you want to hear?" I asked.

"A new story," Clarence said. "Something you haven't told us before."

I laughed. "Are you getting tired of my bedtime stories?"

"No," Richard said, "I just don't want to hear any stories about princesses. What about a story about a prince or a king, or maybe a warrior."

I looked at their five expectant faces. "Ok, I can do that."

I sat down on the edge of the boys' bed and the girls moved to the side of their bed and huddled together.

"Once upon a time, there was a king who had many children, and he was dying, and all his sons wanted to be the next king, but the king knew that his oldest son would not be the best leader for the nation-"

"Why?" Grace asked.

"Well, because he was a proud man, and the leader would have to be humble and wise. So instead, he chose one of his youngest sons to be the king."

"Yeah!" Richard, the youngest of the boys, said. His two brothers rolled their eyes and scowled.

"This son becomes the king, and his father dies not too long after. The new king knows that he needs a lot of help running a whole nation on his own. So, he asks the Lord for a good gift. What do you think that was?"

"Maybe a good military?" Robert asked.

"No, he asked for wisdom."

"Are you telling us the story of Solomon?" Mercy asked. "Sister Evans told us about him asking for wisdom in Sunday School."

"Did she?" I asked. "Well, did she tell you anything else?"

"Only that he made a wise decision with two women fighting about a baby."

"Yes, Solomon did make some wise decisions during his life, but he also made some bad ones."

"But if he was the wisest man, how could he make bad decisions?"

"Sometimes you know what to do, and what not to do, and sometimes you just don't do what is right," I said.

"Has that ever happened to you?" Mercy asked.

"Yes," I nodded. What I didn't say is that it's happening to me right now.

***

When I originally moved to Michigan, I put myself back into the full study of his Word. I reacquainted myself with the Word and prayer, learning how to be attentive to his voice again. I so desperately wanted to hear the voice of the Lord. I even used to pray for Master Marshall and Master Reeves repentance. I prayed quite fervently about this. But I realized over time that this would never happen. Not when the large parts of the nation, not only told them that their practice was acceptable, but that it was the righteous thing to do.

Instead of wasting more time in prayer on useless things, I served in our local church faithfully and gave myself to praying for and helping those who had actually been enslaved. Eventually, I was asked to become the minister of our local church. I worked with others to encourage the church to stand strong in our opposition to slavery. We refused to fellowship with those who promoted this sin. I enjoyed shepherding God's people, and I enjoyed bringing doctrine, reproof, correction, and instruction in righteousness, but oh, how I longed to just hear his voice rouse me from my slumber once more! I started taking in fugitives into the church. I was doing all the right things,

I was successful in the eyes of many, and yet I still just longed to hear his voice.

Yes, I know that God speaks through his Word, and I was thankful for his mercy, that he had not discarded me due to my sin. But I missed the closeness that I once had with him as a child when I could hear his voice so clearly resound inside of me. I could sense that the Lord was at work in our congregation, continuously bringing in fugitives eager to hear the Word after being told a false or incomplete gospel on their plantations.

***

Get up! Go to the Marshall plantation and preach against it because their evil has come up before me.

I remembered the first time I heard that message from the Lord. It had just been a month since I had been voted the pastor of Calvin Township Church. My congregation mostly consisted of new freedmen and mixed native people, neither of them had learned much of the

Bible, but they were open and eager to learn. I devoted my whole life to gathering this group together that often lived well with each other, that is until I met two white abolitionists, Caleb and Josephine Baleine, that wanted to join the church. They had come from a sister church that we had in Canada. We sometimes sent people there if they were desperate to leave the States and be completely free of any capture. The church had been predominantly black and then it was joined by members of the Saponi, Lumbee, and Pamunkey tribes. The free blacks and formerly enslaved blacks all viewed them with suspicion. Were they spies sent from Bourbon and Boone County in Kentucky to trap and send back slaves to their former masters? The South had been aiming to enact the Fugitive Slave Law and people here, including myself, were fearful of what this could mean for us. The native tribes were leerier of white men and what they would do once they found their footing here. They would take over and drive us out, plus many of them had married and had children with black people here.

However, when I spoke with the Baleines, I sensed none of this intention. I tested them for a long while and kept them far away and then at arm's length. One day, they sat in my office, both blond, prim and proper, the wife with her hair neatly pulled back at the nape, dressed in fine clothing.

"So, tell me, why would you want to join Calvin Township Church instead of the many white churches that you all have access to?"

"We do not desire to sit in a church service where there is pretense. Many of the whites here claim to be better than their southern counterparts, but while they may not chain, sell, or whip you, they would not eat with you, let alone invite you in their home for a meal," Caleb responded passionately.

"We want to be where we can actually help and make a difference," Josephine said.

I thought for a moment. "What if your greatest help would be to stay within the white community and work to reach them, since I will never have access to do the work of the gospel there?" I rose from my chair and paced as I thought. "I appreciate your desire for unity, but I worry that it may put my congregation under great scrutiny from the white community. It may put you in a great deal of discomfort. Our congregation is not sure of your intentions."

I did not tell them that I was still unsure of their intentions. I knew what they told me: They were Canadians that had come down to help as conductors. Caleb was a doctor, and his wife was a nurse. They had no children, and they saw the only solution to this issue of slavery was war. They anticipated and welcomed it as a solution.

I called a members' meeting to ask the church if they would be open to welcoming Caleb and Josephine into the body. I was met with resounding outrage. I anticipated fear, I anticipated hesitancy. What I did not anticipate was this. People rose from their pews to let me know that if I welcomed them that this would be akin to opening the gates of destruction into the church. Many told me that if I made this decision that they would no longer remain members.

I prayed long and hard about this decision. I had my fears that the Baleines could be lying to me. I fasted and asked the Lord to lead me to his perfect will. I clung to his words in Corinthians and Ephesians that Christ came to do away with our divisions. If I could just show the members what the Word says, then I'm sure that we could come to an agreement. The next Sunday, I was beginning a sermon on our unity together in Christ, despite our different races and backgrounds when I felt the Word resound in my chest.

Get up! Go to the Marshall plantation and preach against it because their evil has come up before me.

Stunned and disoriented, I stumbled through the rest of my sermon while my heart raced. For so long, I had wanted to hear the Lord's voice. But not this message. I could not go for obvious reasons. At best, I would be enslaved again. Most likely, I would be killed. Torn apart by dogs, burned, whipped, or in some other way, brutalized before the entire plantation. I could not go.

Why would the Lord give me this message? I could not leave my congregation at a time like this to preach to people that did not deserve the care and attention that my congregation needed.

Even if I got a chance to speak, they would not listen to a message of repentance. They never have before, and they never will. I could not go. Why had their sin just come up before God? They have been doing evil for generations. They had sold my father, abused my wife, my mother, and whipped me mercilessly. I had watched them brutally murder people for years. They did not deserve to experience the love and grace of God. They deserved his wrath. They needed to understand the weight of their wickedness. I could not go. I could not go. I would not go.

After the sermon, which I am not sure how I got through, I felt scattered and conflicted. I was sweating and confused. I focused on the faces of the members. They looked unfazed by my words. Several of them just wordlessly got up and shuffled out of the sanctuary. A few came up to tell me their displeasure.

"Pastor Anderson, you're making a big mistake here."

"I can't bring my family here if you put them in danger."

"What about all the runaways that we have safely stowed here, will you risk them too?"

"You bring those white people here and we'll just find us a new pastor!"

"We just voted you in, we can vote you back out!"

I had two dilemmas now. The Lord seemed to be closing in on me on every side. I could listen to my members and refuse visitation and membership to the Baleines. This would make the church happy, even though I felt like it was against scripture. By doing this, I could avoid this ridiculous request to go to the South. My church needed me.

Or I could throw caution to the wind and invite the Baleines into the church. Some members would leave, but perhaps it was all bluff. They would not vote me out. There weren't many other options around. I could weather the storm and avoid the South. In fact, I decided I would use the money I had saved up to help charter a new voyage that the church could take by increasing our efforts to bring even more enslaved people to freedom. Going to the South was impractical, I would do much better by bringing as many souls as possible from the South out of enslavement and here on free soil.

I decided to welcome the Baleines in. Members were not happy and many left. I lost about seventy-five percent of my congregation. However, I felt like I had done the right thing. But every moment of every day, I could not get His voice away from me. There was this weight in my chest. A pounding in my head.

Get up! Go to the Marshall plantation and preach against it because their evil has come up before me.

I cannot go. I cannot go. I will not go.

***

I continued to plunge myself into the depths of the work of the church. I visited those who had left the church and tried to give them assurance and bid them to come back. Some were not angry with me, just merely fearful and said that they were too nervous about getting close to Caleb and Josephine. What if the Baleines learned their faces and names, they would be the first to be rounded up, shackled, and returned to the horrors of their former masters. I told these congregants that I was risking the same fate. This did not really help matters. This seemed to just add to their confusion, and for those who were angry with me, it added fuel to their fury.

If it hadn't been for men who desired to own others like property, who brutalized human beings, sold them, raped them, then we wouldn't be in this mess to begin with. We could live as a church unified by our association with Jesus Christ. Men like Marshall were the cause of so much disorder and pain in our country.

This is why I could never go back there,

never to the Marshall Plantation. But an upheaval began in the Calvin Township Church. One Sunday, as I entered the church, I noticed that all the members who hadn't been here in a while had returned to the house. Initially, I almost smiled in glee, until I noticed the hardness of some of their faces. Many I noticed, could not even look at me. I glanced quickly across the space and noticed that the members maintained a far distance from the Baleines.

A man named Clark stood up and spoke, "Pastor Anderson, we appreciate the fine service you've given to this church from the moment you came, but we feel as though the last few weeks, you've made a huge mistake. You have brought a storm into this place. We fear for our safety, for our families. Perhaps if you are gone, then we can find calm again. We the members have decided that it is best that you no longer serve as our pastor and that the couple in the back would also need to leave as well."

I thought about the boldness that it took them to oust me, but the sheer audacity that it took to oust a white couple as well. Free blacks had power in Cass County, but definitely not as much power as whites.

I stood, stunned. "Is this truly the vote of the majority?" I asked.

I heard a rumbling as voices said "ay".

I nodded my head. "Then I will respect your wishes. Toss me out if you will," I said with offense. "I only have one request. Will you recommend me to our sister church in Canada?" I asked.

Again, the church murmured as they deliberated and said, "ay".

I nodded again and said, "Thank you for your consideration." Some of the men looked at me with pity; others were more than ready for me to leave. I picked up my sermon notes, and my Bible, and I walked down the aisle, out of the church, and away from His presence.

***

Since my arrival in Michigan, my entire life,

my entire being, has been dedicated to the church and the railroad. It had come before anything else; I never sought a wife to divide my time, and I never took a day off. Yet, in the moments that I needed them to trust me, to trust my judgment, they had turned on me. I could understand their distrust of the Baleines, but their distrust of me and my intentions, enough to oust me without so much of a fight, had been painful. I still cared about their well-being even though they were no longer my flock to shepherd. I began to plan my move to Canada. At least there I could officially find peace. I would no longer have to worry about the Fugitive Slave Act. I had enough money saved to get on a boat and be there by the end of the week. As I focused on my packing, night had fallen, and I began to look around for a candle or a lantern.

Get up! Go to the Marshall plantation and preach against it because their evil has come up before me.

"No," I said audibly as I continued to pack my boxes. Just the thought of facing Master

Marshall, made me feel like vomiting. Repentance? All I would want to do is kill him.

There was a knock at the door. Who would be coming at this time of night? I went to look out of the window carefully, when I heard.

"Open up! We know you're in there."

My heart began to race, and I tried to carefully hide myself before I heard the door being kicked in. Before I knew it, three men entered my home and two quickly came and snatched me up. They smelled like they had been traveling without a proper bath in weeks.

The third one approached me with a piece of paper, it was dark, and I could barely see. "Are you Azariah Marshall?" he asked me, pushing the paper in front of me.

I did not answer. He slapped me with his open hand across the face. "Are you Azariah Marshall?" he repeated.

I gathered myself. "My name is Jesse Anderson."

He pulled backwards and said, "Mhmmm. Can you show me your papers?" he asked.

The men holding my arms let me go and I went to my kitchen drawer and retrieved my manumission papers and handed it to him. He looked at it.

"How do I know this is real?" he asked.

"They are," I lied.

The next thing I knew, they began to beat and punch me mercilessly. "How about I rip them up and carry you on back home to Tennessee?" he asked. My body was filled with dread and pain.

"How about I shoot you where you stand for trespassing?" I heard a voice from the door say. I turned to see both Baleines there, shotguns in hand. They didn't even give him an opportunity to answer. Before I knew it, the man was shot, his chest exploding in blood as he crumpled to the floor. The two other men were next. I looked on the floor to see one of their heads blown off, and the other shouting in pain from his shoulder wound. The Baleines stood over the two who were still alive and finished their work.

I threw up and then everything went hazy.

***

"Whither shall I go from thy spirit? or whither shall I flee from thy presence? If I ascend up into heaven, thou art there: if I make my bed in hell, behold, thou art there. If I take the wings of the morning, and dwell in the uttermost parts of the sea; Even there shall thy hand lead me, and thy right hand shall hold me. If I say, Surely the darkness shall cover me; even the night shall be light about me. Yea, the darkness hideth not from thee; but the night shineth as the day: the darkness and the light are both alike to thee."

I whispered the psalm to myself. All I could see initially was darkness. It felt like Hell, absent of God, void of his goodness, filled with loneliness and terror. There was an all-consuming darkness and the scent of rotting flesh. It was there that I saw what I had always thought would bring me great pleasure: it was what appeared to be the figure of Master Marshall and Mr. Reeves. They shrieked and clawed at themselves, tearing at their skin, but as they tore their flesh off muscle and bone, it reappeared, like it was taunting them. It was as if their skin was burning them. Their skin had been what separated them from everyone else, what gave them a license to buy and sell human beings as if they were nothing more than mere livestock. I watched them in their suffering, stunned at the grisly horror of it all. They deserved it. They deserved every bit of it. All the suffering they had inflicted on others and their families, they deserved to spend an eternity like this, without relief.

As I watched them with satisfaction, the Spirit of God whispered to me, *"Azariah, no compassion for the lost?"*

I instantly felt ashamed, and then I was angry. "Should they receive my compassion? They have had none for me, for Honey, Dove, my father, my mother, and the many who have been bought, sold, and brutalized by them."

"Let the wicked forsake his way, and the unrighteous man his thoughts, and let him return unto the Lord, and he will have mercy upon him; and to our God, for he will abundantly pardon."

"They will never repent, Lord. It is useless."

"Generations of this hatred will only yield more hatred," He showed me something to come. In a flash I saw years of more enslavement, what appeared to be a bloody war, men's bodies pierced with hot metal and then the joy of freedom on the faces of my brothers and sisters, followed by the cruelty of white robes, burning crosses, hanging bodies from trees, beaten and mutilated, inequity, mistreatment, and the anger of a million white faces as black boys and girls walked to schools.

I was right. They would never change. But then I saw something else. Their face of hatred morphed into ours. It had a different skin color, but the same look. Then I saw my brothers and sisters like an army of the dead marching towards me, their shrieks matching those of Master

Marshall's and Mr. Reeves. Just like them, they tore at their burning flesh.

"This sin," The Lord said, his voice thick with grief, *"is contagious. It will consume you all."*

I was breathless. We had already suffered so much; I could not stand the sight of more future suffering. Knowing that what the Lord was showing me was not just physical, but spiritual, nearly crushed me. "I must save them."

"Which ones?"

"My people!"

"They are all my children."

I pointed in disgust at Master Marshall and Mr. Reeves, "They are no kin to me! If he had not existed, I would've known freedom. I would've known you sooner."

He directed my gaze back to Marshall as he still agonizingly tore at his flesh. *"He is your blood. Without him, there is no you."*

My body stiffened. Against my will, my eyes began to tear. My anger seemed quelled only by the blow to my heart. How could I have not realized this? People had been hinting at this my whole life. Master Marshall could not be my father. I doubled over in sobs. I knew better than to call the Spirit of God a liar. But I wish he had lied to me. It would've hurt much less.

He knew that I was in pain, and he spoke to me gently, *"Get up, Azariah, go to the Marshall plantation, and preach against it, because their evil has come up before me. I am with you."*

"I told you before, Lord, they will not repent. It is useless."

"The Lord is not slow to fulfill his promise as some count slowness, but is patient toward you, not wishing that any should perish, but that all should reach repentance. Lean not to your own understanding."

"What will I even tell them?"

"The spirit of man is the candle of the Lord, searching all the inward parts of the belly."

And with that I awoke, spewed out of the depths of Sheol, but alive.

***

When I woke up, I realized that I had been brought to a house adorned with heavy drapery that had tassels on the ends. As I moved to sit up, I felt the sharp pain and groaned. A woman, her blond hair pulled back at her nape, quickly came to my side and called out, "Caleb!"

Caleb entered the room, his hair, the color of the golden sand dunes in Michigan. For the first time, I realized their hair reminded me of Master Marshall and his wife. I panicked and flailed, trying to get up despite the pain.

"Lie down. You're safe here," Josephine cooed.

I did not speak nor lie down. I eyed them both suspiciously. "What happened? How did you know about the catchers?"

"They started coming around and asking whites about you. When they came to our house, we started to prepare and trailed them."

"Am I still in Michigan?"

"No, we brought you across. You're on Canadian soil."

I finally laid back. I had made it across.

His wife spoke up now, "You've been so restless. You've been crying out in your sleep."

It was then I knew that even though I had made it across, I would probably not get to enjoy my newfound freedom. If I stayed here, I would still not find peace. As I looked at the Baleines and thought on the events of the last month, I believed that the Lord had sent them here to wreak havoc and the slave catchers to bring me to a place of obedience. If I stayed here in Canada, I think I would just be swallowed by another of life's storms. Only this time, I'm not sure if I would survive it.

The only way back to the South was the same way I had escaped to the North: under the guise of my fair skin. I wondered if I would be more terrified when I traveled North or when I made the trek back to Tennessee. I would pretend to be someone else, and probably most people would forget what Azariah looked like and only believe me to be Jesse Anderson. But I knew that this was not a guarantee. In fact, I found it highly unlikely that they would not recognize me and that this message that the Lord was asking me to bring would surely result in my death. Perhaps, he had a Daniel-type situation in store for me. He could spare my life even if they threw me in the lions' den. Or perhaps my namesake would help me and no matter what fiery furnace they threw me in, I would survive. I did not know. It was the unknown that fueled my fear.

I could not go to the South with the message the Lord had given me. There were no abolitionists in the South. All of them had fled North for a reason. Even a white man preaching abolition could be subject to death.

Caleb interrupted my thoughts, "You can start fresh here."

"I have to go back."

"You can't go back to Michigan. They are looking for us all. They will kill us on sight."

"No, you don't understand. I must go back to the South to my former plantation to settle some business."

Caleb and Josephine's brows both

furrowed in deep confusion. "You're right. I do not understand why you would risk certain death. Do you have a family that you must rescue?" Josephine asked.

"No. My family is all gone. The Lord gave me a word for the owner of my plantation. I must deliver it to him."

"Even if it requires your life?" Caleb asked incredulously.

"Yes," I said, "Even if it requires my life."

Over the next few days, Caleb, Josephine and I talked at length about my return to Tennessee. They hoped to change my mind. Caleb even had an idea that instead of me returning to preach to Marshall, that I could go back to exact revenge on Marshall. I could picture it. I could go back and work with the kitchen staff to make sure that he saw his end, or I could go down there with Caleb and make sure that he experienced what the slave catchers that came for me did. I was eager to say yes to Caleb. It made more sense to. But if what happened to me with the slave catchers was any indication of what would happen if I continued to resist the Lord, then I was hesitant to join Caleb. I decided to do one last thing against the recommendation of Caleb and Josephine.

I fasted and prayed fervently. I desperately prayed that the Lord would change his mind. Caleb and Josephine recommended that I eat so that I could recover well from my injuries. Two days into my fast, my bruises had already stopped hurting and began to lighten up. Even Josephine noted this was remarkable, given the severity of the beating. On the third day, I heard his voice again as I sat in my room praying that the Lord would, instead of the Marshalls, bring the Baleines closer to him.

Get up! Go to the Marshall plantation and preach against it because their evil has come up before me.

I don't know why, but I sensed this time that if I did not heed, there would not be the same mercy I had received when I was rescued from the clutches of slave catchers. I took the time Caleb and Josephine recommended for me to get well. Over the time I spent with them in recovery, about two weeks in total, I learned a great deal about them. They had trouble conceiving children, and instead of going through the heartbreak of another miscarriage, they dedicated themselves to the cause of abolition. They had grown tired of waiting for the U.S. government to come to its senses legislatively and waiting on the Lord to end their personal suffering and to end the suffering of others. They hadn't initially set out to accomplish this justice by violence, but they had grown disillusioned with diplomatic talks with slave owners that seemed to go nowhere. The attitudes of enslavers who claimed to know God but did acts of atrocities against other human beings had made them question their own faith. They explained to me that the only thing that had kept them remotely tethered to the faith had been that we as the formerly enslaved still managed to believe despite our own suffering. They could not understand it. Yet, they yearned for faith like that, even though they admitted that they did not possess it. It was why they truly wanted to join my church. My former church.

We spent a great deal of time talking about my life before and after I became free. I told them about my life on the Marshall Plantation. I told them how I had been chosen to be the preacher, how my father had been sold away, how Francesca and I married, about Dove, and about my mother. One night after dinner, the three of us sat discussing the situation in the US, surrounded by lamplight and the glowing candelabras.

"Are you sure that the Lord spoke to you, Jesse? Doing this would almost certainly mean death," Josephine said. I knew she had grown to see me as a brother and a friend and was deeply concerned about my wellbeing.

"I am sure."

Caleb interjected, "But how do you know that it was the Lord's voice? Do you really think that he even speaks to us or interferes in our daily lives? If he did, why hasn't he brought justice to your people?"

"I do not know why he has not changed

our plight yet. Sometimes the Lord works much more slowly than I'd like him to. But I do know that this is his voice, or I would be back in Michigan enjoying my freedom, instead of putting my life at risk."

"Your former master will not listen to you," Josephine said with certainty.

I nodded, "I know."

"So why are you going?" she asked.

"I told you. I must be obedient to the Lord." I pursed my lips. "I agree with you. This makes no sense, and they will not repent. I know that the Lord is a gracious God, but he…" I tried to find my words. I had spent time already trying to share the gospel with them. "I know I spoke with you about how the Lord died for every sin and will forgive any sin. But the Marshalls… they don't have any goodness in them. They wouldn't even know how to respond to the call of God to repent". I started to respond to my own questions. "This must be a test. All this time I've prayed for the destruction of that evil place and those evil people, and The Lord wants me to witness it up close and not from afar. I'll go and tell Marshall the message to repent, and he'll refuse and then judgment will come. I think the Lord is finally allowing me to witness it."

Caleb looked at me with pity in his eyes. "I pray that you are right," he said, as he got up, went into a drawer, and handed me a revolver. "Take it, in case you're wrong."

***

As soon as I felt physically strong enough, I boarded a train heading South. The further south I traveled, the more my paranoia grew. This time I rode in the whites only section of the train, and I became convinced that as people looked at me, their glances were filled with suspicion. For most of the ride, I kept my eyes down, reading a Bible or newspaper.

It had not been long after we arrived in Kentucky that I heard a voice near me ask, "Are you a preacher?"

Startled, I looked up to see a teenage boy

with glasses looking down at me.

"Yes," I affirmed, wanting to look back down, but remembering that by looking away from a young white boy's gaze may give away my true identity. Only a slave would be forced to divert their gaze. A white man would have full liberty to look into the eyes of someone he was speaking to.

The boy continued. "I figured when I saw you reading that Bible. Most men probably read a page or two, but you were reading it like it was any ol' book."

I chuckled nervously. "Yes, well I always have to be in preparation for what The Lord would have me say."

"Does God really talk to people? I mean in a voice like how I'm talking to you?"

I thought for a moment. "I used to think he didn't. But now, I think he does."

He nodded his head pensively. "Sure would like to have that experience some day. I'm not wanting to be a preacher or anything, but I think it would be nice to know what God sounded like." He shook off his thoughts and spoke. "Sorry to bother you, sir." He extended his hand to me. "Have a good one, Reverend."

"It wasn't a bother at all," I said, and fished through my bag. "I have another Bible in here," I said, "He speaks through this as well," I said, handing it to him.

He smiled and nodded his head. "Thank you, sir."

Unlike this boy, I wish I had never heard him speak to me. The weight of the responsibility that rushed from that voice was too much. When hearing his voice, one was required to obey that voice. What if this boy grew up to hear he needed to travel around the South encouraging men to support the efforts of the North to unify the country under abolition? Would he think it were God or the devil speaking to him? Even if he knew it was God, how would he change something that went against everything he had ever been taught about his life and the lives of others?

I mulled over the conversation that I had

with Caleb and Josephine the night before I left and the look of pity on both of their faces. This message that the Lord wanted me to bring made no sense. It would not be listened to, let alone adhered to. It was then that I made up my mind. I would not tell them to repent because they were slave owners. It was neither logical nor plausible. I would simply tell them to repent and then I would accomplish what the Lord had told me to do, and I could retreat back to the North as quickly as possible before anyone noticed who I was. In fact, it might be best to dress as a homeless beggar or a madman. That way I could possibly escape death. That was exactly what I did when I hit the border of Tennessee.

After I exited the train, I wanted to stick to the mental map of what I designed on the train ride down. I needed to come across as a crazed, homeless man, but I needed to make sure I had transportation to get out of there as soon as I brought the message to them. Originally, I had wanted to stay a bit to see the judgment of the Lord rain down on them. Would it come down like on Sodom and Gomorrah? My curious mind raced with these thoughts, but I decided to stick to the best plan of safety that I could come up with now that I was already in Tennessee.

I bought a horse and traveled a bit each day, plopping myself down at some town square, yelling, "Repent, lest our great state of Tennessee be brought down!" Oftentimes people laughed and disregarded me. They thought I was a crazed man or drunk, and I realized that perhaps for my safety, I should play into their assumptions. So, I would find empty bottles of liquor on the street and pretend that I had just finished drinking it as I told people to repent. Sometimes, I was spat on, other times women and some men would bend down to drop a coin at my feet, their eyes filled with pity. I would often go out to the woods and sleep under trees, looking up at the night sky, using my coins only to buy food.

Each day, I rode a couple miles, inching my way closer to the Marshall plantation. Each day, my heart grew colder towards these people, these brutish people who had not an ounce of compassion. If they knew me to be a poor black soul begging for change, I would've been dead long ago. The only pity they had for me was that they thought that their fellow white brother had fallen into hard times, and even then, most could care less about me.

I kept moving towards the plantation, and finally, after three days, the plantation was in sight. If it was daytime, I was sure I would be recognized, but I came prepared for that prospect. Just to feel a sense of security, I reached down to touch the firearm that Caleb had given me. I waited until nightfall and made my way to the slave quarters at the Marshall Plantation. Everything looked the same as I had left it twenty years ago. The shacks for the slaves looked more worn, but everything was still in its place. There was still the smell of earth, and I didn't know if it was my imagination, but I felt like I could smell the stench of blood and sweat. The sound of the cicadas felt like it was roaring in my ears, and I took one last look up at the sky and prayed. For the first time I was grateful to see this place again, knowing I would see it destroyed soon. *Lord, let your will be done.*

I led my horse away to not arouse the eyes of the overseers or anyone else who might be doing rounds at night. Slowly and quietly, I started to make my way closer to the slave quarters. I knocked on Chloe and George's door. I hoped this was still her door. George opened the door, and his eyes moved from confusion to shock. George was a good two to three inches shorter than me. Once I knew that he recognized me, I covered his mouth and pushed my way inside of the shack, closing the door with one foot. I released George from my grip and he and Chloe stood there, their eyes wide with fear.

"Azariah?" George asked. When I had left years ago, he and Chloe's hair only had a few grays in it. Now the gray seemed to have taken over George's head and was on its way to consuming Chloe's hair. Both were probably close to fifty now.

"Yeah, it's me," I whispered.

Chloe stepped forward and touched my

face tenderly, "It really is you. You look like you been through, Azariah." She examined my dirty face and clothes. "Why you back here?"

"Too much to explain. Where's Master Marshall?"

"And you talkin' like you ain't from 'round here," she said. I sense both a statement and a warning to her assessment of me. She sighed and then said, "He asleep."

"What you lookin' for him for?" George asked.

"I jus' gotta talk to him," I said.

"I thought you looked like you done lost yo' mind. I guess I was right," George said.

"I ain't here cause I wanna be. I have a message I must give him, that's all."

"Unless that message got something to do with that gun you got, then you looking to die. Master Marshall been on a mission to find you and Meadow for a long time and just when I think he done gave up, you show up," Chloe said. Her dark skin was highlighted in moonlight.

Meadow? I tried to remember that name.

"You talking about Mara's daughter?" I asked. "She escaped?"

George cocked his head to one side, confused. "You don't know….?"

Chloe spoke up, "Mmm hmm."

"Mara," I whispered. "I remember now. I told her I would try to come back for Meadow." I knew that I had lied to her. At the time, I think Mara also knew I was lying to her. "Where is she?" I asked.

Chloe cleared her throat. "Mara died." "What? Was she sick? What happened?"

"Meadow needed more time to get North. Mara made sure that she got that time. She tried to poison Mistress Marshall and her daughter. They sent the dogs after her. But I think that's what Mara wanted, if the dogs were on her, then they couldn't be huntin' Meadow."

I closed my eyes. I hated every part of this place. I hated that the Lord had sent me back here. I didn't want to hear these stories. I spent twenty years as a refugee to make sure that I never had to see this place or any place like it again. "Did she make it North?" I asked.

George spoke up, "Yeah, she made it," he said, as he moved over to lean on the wall. "Almost killed us all, but she made it. Now, why are you back here? You come to get us all killed too?"

I shifted nervously. "This is gonna sound crazy, but I got a message from God for Marshall and Reeves. I gotta give it to them, and then I'll leave."

George laughed. "Like Chloe said, if that message don't got something to do with that gun, then you must be lookin' to die and to take us with you, by showing up here at night."

Chloe looked serious. "What did the Lord tell you to say?"

George stared at Chloe. "You listenin' to this foolishness? Chloe don't start with those dreams again. I told you-"

Chloe rolled her eyes and then turned back to me. "What did he tell you to say?"

"The spirit of man is the candle of the Lord, searching all the inward parts of the belly."

Chloe smiled. "I didn't think it was time yet. I thought it would be a woman. A girl."

"What are you talking about?"

"Judgement. The Lord showed it to me. I've been praying and he showed it to me. The candle on Master Marshall's golden stick."

I felt true hope for the first time. God would destroy this place, and he chose me to witness it. "You think the Lord is going to destroy this place?"

"Yes, but it didn't look like this. I don't know, maybe I saw it all wrong," she said, confused.

Her doubt frustrated me. I wanted assurance. I swallowed my fear and annoyance all at once. "Chloe, just go on over to Master Marshall and tell him George is sick, and he need to come to see him-"

"Master Marshall ain't coming over here for that," Chloe retorted. "And I know you don't want to just see an overseer come in here."

George interjected, "He gon' think we

helped you do this."

I stared at them first and realized what I would have to do. "Tie me to your chair. Tell him that I came to your cabin and that you overpowered me and held me so that you could turn me over to him."

They both looked at me with an air of suspicion. "You really willing to do that? Knowing that he gon' kill you?" George asked.

"He gon' kill me regardless. No need to get y'all killed along with me. This will get you in his good graces. Maybe an extra nice meal or even some more rest from work."

They stared at me for a moment and then turned to each other. Neither of them said a word and then Chloe turned to me. "We've watched yo' ma and pa taken from us, and now you want us to be responsible for you? Yo' ma would be turnin' in her grave."

I hadn't thought about how Chloe and George would feel about this. I hadn't considered that others besides myself and Honey had possibly mourned for my parents.

"I'm sorry," I said. "If ma is looking down on us, I hope she will blame this all on me. You ain't have nothin to do with us. But this is the only way that I can keep you safe right now. Tie me up and call Master Marshall. Whatever is God's plan, I pray that you are spared from any harm. May it all fall on the guilty." I sincerely hoped that the guilty party was the ones who resided in their comfortable homes built by the labor, pain, and suffering of others.

Chloe took her lamp with her and left the room while George took my gun and then went for something to tie me with. I sat on the chair and waited silently for him.

God, I wished I had died on the way here.

As George started to tie my arms and legs, I heard him begin to sing softly:

My Father, how long?

My Father, how long?

My Father, how long?

Poor sinner suffer here?

I wanted to sing with him the next part, but I realized that even though I used to sing this along with everyone, I don't think I ever believed it. So, George sang it for me.

> *And it won't be long.*
> *And it won't be long.*
> *And it won't be long.*
> *Poor sinner suffer here.*

It seemed an eternity before I saw Master Marshall enter the cabin, the amber light from his torch lighting one side of his face while the other side remained hidden in the shadows. He came in and looked at me with such disbelief, as if he were seeing a ghost or as if he had dreamed of this moment so many times and scarcely believed that it would ever come true. He looked different than I remembered him. He was a bit disheveled, as if he were trying to hold it together but could not. His hair, which was once always cut and combed, was now longer, and he appeared that he hadn't shaved for a few days. Behind him, like an apparition, stood Mr. Reeves with a long, tapered candle. They both shuffled inside quietly, their lights glowing in the darkness of the cabin, the sounds of the night filled in the silence.

"Azariah," Master Marshall said shakily. He took another step forward towards me. My body began to tremble. He stood there examining my face in the dim light. Then he said resolutely, "It really is you. I thought maybe they had just found the wrong person. I have been praying that I would find you for the longest time." He stepped forward and stood right over me. Reeves stood back, his face stone-like with shock. Even he feared what would happen next to me.

I did not speak. Fear gripped me, and I thought of all I could say. I could tell them that salvation comes only from the Lord or give them all the scriptures I knew that showed that slavery was evil.

I felt a fierce blow to my face. The pain from it would have sent me and the chair I was tied to on the ground had it not been for George's body behind me, keeping me from falling.

"Do you know how long I've been

searching for you, boy?!" His face was less than an inch from mine as he screamed, unhinged, his spit spraying onto my face. It was then I found my courage. No, it was not really courage. It was rage. A fearsome yell rose from my belly, burned in my chest and then forced its way to my lips.

"Forty days!" I screamed in the same way he had, spit spraying back on him. "Forty days and this plantation will be destroyed by God almighty himself!"

I expected him to descend on me, showering me with blows, but instead he recoiled. I continued to yell, my self-control gone. "Woe unto him that buildeth his house by unrighteousness, and his chambers by wrong; that useth his neighbor's service without wages, and giveth him not for his work." I looked over at Mr. Reeves, "Tell him the Word! You wouldn't let us read the whole thing, but do you read it? And he that stealeth a man, and selleth him, or if he be found in his hand, he shall surely be put to death. God will have his vengeance on you both! Forty days!"

Master Marshall backed away from me. Mr. Reeves looked stricken with something that I could not quite understand at the time. I thought it to be terror, but now I know that it was the fear of God, the one that, to my dismay, leads to repentance. A thick cloak of silence enveloped everyone in the cabin. George and Chloe stood off to the side, their eyes wild with terror. Master Marshall and Master Reeves' eyes were wide as well, but filled with tears.

Master Reeves broke the silence. "Thus, saith the Lord," he whispered.

These were not the words I was expecting. I was expecting death. I was expecting to figure out how I could physically overpower them and maybe escape once more. That God would allow this to happen seems surreal to me and nonsensical. Neither Master Marshall nor Mr. Reeves struck me again. Instead, Master Marshall turned to Reeves, shaking, his body stiff as he abruptly left. Reeves looked just as shocked as I was, but he said nothing to me as he quickly turned and followed Marshall outside.

Once both of them were out of the cabin, Chloe approached me slowly, "Was this the message you had for them? What about the candle?" she said, her hands trembling as they came down on my forearm.

"The candle does not matter. This is the true message; forty days and this place will be laid waste. God has heard our cries," I said to her. It was partially true. I knew God intended this place for judgment, but the other part about their repentance was too impossible to utter.

Chloe covered her mouth and looked at George. "It didn't look like this, I don't know. Azariah, are you sure? I know I saw a woman coming and she had the candle stick. But maybe you're right, maybe this is it."

George still looked like he was frozen in time. He finally shook his head. "We'll all be whipped for this."

Chloe chastised him, "You have no faith. This could be our moment. Just like the time Azariah taught us about Moses carryin' all them people to freedom."

I nodded. "You remembered."

She gave me a small smile. "I'd tell myself the story over and over so that I wouldn't forget."

A tear trailed down my face. "They tried to keep the Word from us, but the Word always prevails." Chloe reached down and started to move towards the bindings on my arm. "No, leave them," I said. "They'll be back. If they see that you've untied me, they'll punish you."

By order, George and Chloe kept me confined in their home through the night. The rope had now begun to blister my skin, and had it not been for the terror of what type of torture Marshall would devise to make an example out of me, I would've slept from exhaustion. Chloe and George had retired to bed for the night, while I sat bound. I thought about speaking to God, but I am unsure if my fear or my anger kept me from doing so. All night long, I thought about the fact that Master Marshall was going to bring me in front of the whole plantation and kill me. All I could think about were the many ways that he could do it. When I wasn't thinking of that, I thought about the absurdity of God's Word, that this man who had bound me in slavery, and still bound me now, deserved an ounce of mercy. The sound of the soft breeze and cicadas once was a peaceful lull to sleep. But now, my heart pounded, my body fluctuated between hot and cold. I felt perspiration gathering under my arms. In truth, it was all over my body.

After many hours, I had finally fallen asleep, I did not hear when both Chloe and George had woken up and left the cabin. Chloe jolted me awake, whispering frantically. "They called a fast, Azariah. *A fast.*"

I was still gathering my bearings, and my body was still extremely groggy. "They told us to untie you and let you go."

"*Let me go?*" I said in disbelief.

"Yes," George said assuredly.

Was this a trick? Did they plan on shooting me as I walked out? Were there dogs waiting outside to tear into my flesh?

"They said, you can go if you'd like, or that you can stay as a guest."

"A guest?!" I said loudly. Chloe nodded. "Yes, that's what they said."

I thought about leaving, but my curiosity about what would come next kept me there. If I left, would I subject everyone else to mass punishment? I could not stomach it. If they were going to unleash their fury, I'd rather them just kill me and be done with it. I was welcome to stay in better quarters, but instead I decided to remain in one of the slave quarters.

The first day, I watched from the porch as all the women that worked in the house walked in lines carrying chicken, ham, greens and all the fixings to the different cabins. People came out of their cabins, gawking in disbelief. All the food that would normally belong to the Marshalls now was given to us as they fasted.

Some people ate, some turned down the meal, fearful that this was a test of loyalty and allegiance from Master Marshall. We were also told that we were not commanded to work. This also set off widespread bewilderment. Some enjoyed the rest their bodies never had the luxury of having. Some, not knowing anything else other than forced servitude, went back out into the fields to work, afraid that Master Marshall would change his mind, or, as some said, he would "come to his senses".

Those who went out to work were further surprised when he came in the evening to pay them their wages for a day of work. By day two, you could hear songs of praise rising from the shacks to the fields.

On day three, I received a knock on my door shortly after dawn. Mistress Marshall and her son, who was now a young teenager (my guess was about the age of 13) were at the door. Their faces were fixed with disgust as they beheld me. We stood there for what seemed like minutes, although I'm sure it was seconds, as they glared at me. I did not break eye contact with her, even though I knew that this insolence was a capital offense.

"Ma'am," I said, trying to break the silence.

She swiftly slapped me across the face with as much force as she could muster.

My face stung. I turned and composed myself and once again faced her.

"You may have put some sort of spell on my husband, but I am not beguiled!" She said as her face reddened.

"I can assure you that I have not put any spell on anyone. What is happening here is…." I struggled to find the words. "It is nauseating to me."

Both seemed taken aback by my statement. "Why did you come here?" her son finally asked.

"I came to do one thing," I said, "Which is to watch the judgment of God fall on this place," I spoke directly to Mistress Marshall. "Your husband may try to feign this 'repentance', but if he thinks that decades of sin will just be wiped away, he is sadly mistaken."

Master Marshall's son lunged at me and his mother stood in front of him, holding her hand firmly to his chest, commanding him to stay. She took a deep breath and then began to shake her head in disbelief, before she turned back to me. "I should've let you die. Your mother was a thorn in my side. I thought my sorrows would be gone when she died, and now I see that unless I crush every part of her, including her seed, that she will always haunt me."

Fear filled me, that she was able to say this with such a calm demeanor. I knew she was serious. "Your husband has called a fast. Should you two not be joined with him and your daughter in prayer. Would you defy your husband and have me killed?"

"My husband is not well right now and once this community sees it; they'll do something about all of this...and you."

"Count your days, boy," her son said and then they turned and left.

I knew that I needed to get out of this place as quickly as possible. I packed up all my belongings in a hurry. But just as I was getting my horse ready, the overseer came out and told me that Master Marshall and Master Reeves were requesting a meeting with us. Usually, we were ordered to a meeting and told if we weren't there right away, then the whip would be across our back. But this time, it seemed as though he pleaded with us to grace him with our presence. It was all very bizarre, not just to me, but to everyone listening. I knew that it might be best to leave the plantation altogether right away, but my curiosity got the best of me.

With apprehension, we filed to our usual meeting spot, a place near a large oak tree where many times we had been called to be told that our quota had gone up or to watch someone whipped for something they had done or failed to do. Our eyes looked as they usually did whenever we were summoned here, wide and roaming. We noticed that Mr. Reeves' slaves were there as well. This added to the strangeness indeed. Soon Master Marshall and Mr. Reeves joined us outside. Mistress Marshall and her children remained on the porch. I noticed that her face was set in stone with defiance and anger as she held her teenage son and daughter close to her.

Master Marshall took off his hat and with a trembling hand he combed his fingers through his hair. He still hadn't shaved. He looked out at all of us with red-rimmed, watery eyes, and swallowed hard. *Could it be? No, he would never. It could never be.*

He cleared his throat, but it did not change his quivering voice. "Many of you have worked here for a long time. Some your whole lives. You have been here since I was a boy. Your work has given me all that I own. And I have treated you with contempt. No, I have treated you with disgrace. I have done things that has cost lives. I have taken your children from you. I have… I have violated the women who were under my household." His eyes were bloodshot now and he struggled to speak. "I repent and I pray for God's mercy on my soul. I do not deserve it. But I ask for it nonetheless."

The wind rustled the leaves in the trees, squirrels scurried by, as we stood there in silence. I glanced at Mistress Marshall as she stared at Master Marshall with pure hatred. Our once wide, roaming eyes were now fixed on Master Marshall. Large eyes, mouths agape, we just stared. Mr. Reeves finally spoke, "We do not deserve your forgiveness, and we do not have enough to pay you back for all that you have lost. What we offer you now may further put you in danger, but it is all we have."

Master Marshall spoke again, "As of this day, none of you will be owned by me, and I pray you're never owned again. I will try my very best to offer you safe passage to the North. Once there, you may start your lives afresh." He nervously grabbed a paper in his pocket. "Reeves and I have been working on a plan. We will go out in different groups. We must go in different directions to avoid being caught. Reeves and I plan on going with you, and so will the overseers. We won't ask you to risk your lives if we are not willing to risk ours. If you choose to stay here on this plantation, you may," he stopped and then corrected himself. "No, you *will* be compensated."

Mrs. Marshall stormed back inside the

house, dragging her children with her. Master Marshall looked after them with sorrow and then turned to the rest of us still standing there, nodded his head, put on his hat and walked back inside his house.

The buzz of excitement that started to build in the people around me filled me with anger. Did he really think that this would grant him forgiveness from us? From God? That this would suffice for all that he had done? All the years of misery, all the years of pain and loss. All wiped away with one confession and a shoddy plan for restitution.

I knew I should leave, but I stayed put, partially because I was in shock and partially to try to see all of this to the end. Lord, there must be some judgment to come. Surely, you would not bring me all this way to watch him *actually* repent.

Over the next few days, the plantation was whirling with plans. People had neatly separated themselves into groups of thought. Some were incredulous and excited to head north. Others decided they would stay here, that Marshall hadn't really met the Lord, but had instead lost his entire mind and that they were better off under a new Master. If anyone found out what was happening on this plantation, that Marshall planned on paying his slaves, no, former slaves, there would be hell to pay. Slave owners around here would think his behavior was a disease that would spread.

I remained at the plantation in the room Marshall had given me. Marshall at times seemed like he wanted to talk with me but often held his eyes down in shame. Mistress Marshall, I heard, was a nervous wreck. She still tried to demand the women and men in the house around, but to no avail. Master Marshall would have none of it. Chloe told me that she pitied this woman who had treated her and my mama like trash their whole lives.

"She don't know any better, Azariah," Chloe said.

"She knows plenty," I said with little care. "Judgment for her as well."

"Be careful of all this judgment you ready to dish out, Azariah. Some might spill on you," she said. "Mistress Marshall ain't a nice woman by any means. She done some terrible things to us ladies, but she's also had to sit back and have her husband ignore her at every turn and lay up with woman after woman, on and off this plantation. She don' lost many children before and after those two chillun' she got."

"And she's sold off children from their mothers, and had women beaten for being raped by her husband," I yelled. "You can go ahead and pity her, but I will not. If it were up to her, all of you would be back to work and I would be dead."

Chloe shook her head sadly. "There's much I can't tell you because you wouldn't understand. I don't know if you could understand..." she said, and her voice trailed off. "I know there were many things your mother did not share with you but just know that Mrs. Marshall is the reason you are still alive." She left swiftly before I asked any more questions. How could she leave after making a statement like that? I tried to get Chloe to explain it to me, but she only said, "You'd have to ask the Marshalls yourself."

It was one day before the groups would move out at night. Some were heading West, some to Canada and others to Philadelphia or New York. There was a knock at my door around noontime, and I opened it to find Marshall standing outside. I noticed how the blue of the sky contrasted with his golden locks underneath his signature tan hat.

"Azariah, may I come in?" he asked.

I stared at him and did not answer. I was deciding whether I should say no. I did not want him to speak to me, or worse, beg for my forgiveness. I decided to step aside and let him enter. It felt powerful having him at my mercy. He removed his hat and stepped inside.

"I won't belabor this. I thank you for your word from the Lord."

I planted my feet, and my jaw tightened. "Nothing has changed. This place will be destroyed."

He nodded. "If it must go, then it must." He stepped towards the door. "Azariah, I am responsible for most of the suffering you have experienced. I am responsible for things I don't even know how to speak of."

Initially, I thought he must have been referring to the beatings or to my father being sold away, but I sensed in this moment he was talking of unspoken things. "What are you talking about?"

He looked away in shame, his voice thick and quivering. "Your mama was given to me as a child, to be my servant, but she was my friend, she was sweet and kind, and I… I was enamored by her. My father was not happy about our friendship. I thought your mother was the most beautiful girl. That's why I named her Venus." Tears started to run down his face. "As I grew older, I knew the way I felt for your mother would not be accepted. So, I kept your mother as a servant even when I got married to Anna. Anna was chosen for me. Her father was wealthy and the money that I would inherit from the marriage helped me build all of this."

"So, are you telling me that you loved my mother and not your own wife?" I asked angrily.

He wiped his nose. "Maybe when I was a child, I loved her. Because I still viewed her as my equal in a way. The older I got; I started to tell her that I owned her and that she had to spend time with me. I was angry when she was with others, when she fell in love with someone else. I don't think how I treated your mother was love and she knew it. Your mother couldn't love someone who viewed her as property, so every time I came to her with how I felt, she told me that all she could offer me was a friendship at best."

I stared at him, anger beginning to boil underneath my skin.

"Anna didn't like that I called her Venus, she insisted that I name her Ruth instead." It finally dawned on me that Mrs. Marshall had always called my mother Ruth, not Venus. "I thought marrying Anna would help me to not feel the lust I felt for your mother."

"I don't want to hear this," I said, turning away from him.

"I must confess!" he cried in misery. "I am a scoundrel, and I am a monster." He sank down to the ground. "I am sorry that it is my blood that flows through your veins and not the man that I sold. He had more virtue in one finger than I have in my whole body. Your mother was so distraught at what I had done, that she nearly killed herself when she discovered she was with child. Anna stopped her before she could cause more damage to herself. You were born and your ma never had another child again because of what happened. It's my fault!" He said, agonizing over the words he proclaimed. "Every bit of it."

This information was not new. I had heard the Lord tell me this, but hearing the details, and hearing it from Marshall's own mouth, made my blood boil. He stood kneeling at my feet, and I knew that I could beat until until the skin flailed off his back. I could expose muscle and even bone. I could have him torn apart by dogs, then strung from the oak tree, and burned. Even then, it wouldn't feel like it was enough. I could use this opportunity to do what I've wanted to do for so many years. But instead, I forcefully gritted these words out of my teeth: "I hope you spend the rest of your days in torment. I hope your light gets snuffed out faster than it takes to blow out a candle. Get out. Now."

He shakily stood up, put his hat on his head, and I never saw Marshall ever again.

***

I left immediately after Marshall made his confession. I went back to Michigan the same way I had escaped the first time. I returned to my two-bedroom home. Anger became a part of the floorboards, the blue wallpaper, the windows of my soul. That God would even grant them forgiveness and salvation after all they had done made my entire body burn from the inside out. That thought festered in my soul, and I thought to myself that I would see to it that I would help end slavery since neither the President, nor Congress, nor the Lord were willing to do what needed to be done. All these years I had prayed for slaveholders to change, to repent. It was useless. My only prayer now was that they would meet their reckoning.

At first, I donated money to John Brown's cause. He was building up weaponry, knowing a standoff between the North and South would soon result in war.

When Caleb first saw me return safely, he looked at me with wonder. Josephine cried tears of joy, exclaiming how worried she had been that I was dead. Both described my return as an utter miracle. My return to their house, allowed us time to finally put together our plan on exacting revenge on enslavers. We would visit plantations in border states, usually a slave owner with some sort of debt, most of them due to gambling or mismanagement, and we would offer to buy some of their slaves, so that they could settle their debts. But just freeing some slaves was not enough for me. These men would just go and collect more slaves, so I decided the only way to truly solve this issue would be to free slaves and remove the slave owner completely.

I remembered the plants my mom would tell me to steer clear of and berries she warned about. On each plantation, we arranged to work with a house slave that worked in the kitchen to help poison all the owners, wives, and overseers and then in the moment of their weakness; I helped to kill all of them before disappearing into the night with whomever was brave enough to follow me North. The first time we did this, my heart nearly beat out of my chest, especially as the family started to react to the poison. I'll never forget the Johnson family. They were the first family. I had moved to kill the master and the overseer, and I felt conviction, especially as his wife pleaded with me. I couldn't do it. Caleb had to. I stood outside vomiting until Caleb came and found me and then I heard the wife and her children crying. It took me some time to build the nerve to try again, but each time, it became easier. I reasoned that it was a necessary evil. If I wanted these brothers and sisters I'd freed to remain free, then I needed to kill. The wife and children left behind were better off. With every master I killed, I felt like I was doing what God should have done. I was freeing the oppressed and punishing the oppressor. This is what he should've told me to do to Marshall. Not lead him to mercy.

One year after my visit to the Marshall plantation, I received a letter written by a man in Philadelphia that had married one of the women from the plantation that had escaped with Marshall. He had been a freeman his whole life and knew how to read and write well. His wife had insisted on finding where I was so that she could thank me for coming back to the plantation so that they could be free. At first the letter had warmed my heart, until I realized that she was also giving praise to God for how he had used Marshall and Reeves to bring about their freedom as well. In the letter, her husband dictated what his wife told him about the fate of those who had left the plantation that day.

Marshall and several different teams headed North. They had gone under the guise of a Master relocating with his slaves. He had papers for all of them, and so they had gone undetected for many miles. However, people along the way had noticed the kindness with which Marshall and Reeves had been treating their supposed slaves and suspicion and rumors began to spread. Marshall's team reached Missouri when they were discovered. A group of white men surrounded a house alongside the railroad where they had stopped for rest and food. Marshall protected the conductor and the cargo by keeping everyone hidden under the floorboards of the house, and though the men tried as hard as they could to torture Marshall to get him to give up the location of the people, he kept insisting that he had freed them already and that it was too late. In the end, the men gave up their search but made sure to make an example of Marshall. He was beaten, maimed, shot, and hung. Before he died, he was heard saying, "Lord Jesus, forgive them, they do not understand.

Receive my spirit, Lord." Reeves hadn't been captured but had grown ill on the route. Miraculously, no one ever became sick from his infirmity. I read that he had also prayed as he passed, asking the Lord to watch over the safe passage of everyone still heading north, smiling and telling those with him in his final hours that he could see the Lord. He was grateful that despite his sin, that God had mercy on his soul.

The wife of the husband who had written to me believed that one day she would see both men in heaven and her faith in Jesus had begun after seeing the radical transformation in these men. From what I knew, both Marshall's and Reeves' plantations back in Tennessee had been burned to the ground. People in the area believed that there must've been some curse on the place to make those two men think that a slave should be free. They believed that one of the slave women had conjured up something and had gone on a witch hunt looking for who it could be. Marshall's wife had only managed to retain a few loyal women. Some who had remained on the Marshall plantation had escaped. Others had been sold off to nearby plantations and a few had perished.

I was happy that the plantations had been largely destroyed, but the possibility that I could share a heaven with Marshall and Reeves made me sick.

***

It was a crisp autumn day in October as Caleb; Josephine and I approached another plantation in Kentucky. Remington Manor.

Caleb spoke, "I've gathered some information about John Remington. His house is stockpiled with weaponry, so our first course of action is to gain entrance to the kitchen staff."

Josephine asked, "How will we gain their trust?"

"I know a way," I said with confidence. "Don't worry, I will speak with them. You just focus on earning Remington's trust as a potential buyer."

Caleb had been corresponding via mail with Remington. He was in dire need to sell some of his slaves, due to a gambling debt that he hoped that his wife and father-in-law would not discover. He would try to quickly sell to us to get out of his predicament before his wife could learn of the severity of his debt. As far as his wife knew, we would just be guests for the next two days as her husband worked on a business deal with Caleb. I was to play the part of his right-hand man. I suggested that I play the part of the Baleine's slave to gain easier trust and access to the other slaves, but the Baleine's did not want to treat me as their slave, they said.

When we arrived, we were placed in our own bedrooms and showed a great deal of hospitality. Remington Manor had about ten slaves in total. Seven worked in the field while three women remained in the house. Mrs. Remington took a quick liking to Josephine, and while the two women were together, Remington and Caleb spent time bartering. I closely watched the house slaves to discern who was in charge. I realized after some time that it was a thin woman, named Leona, her hair pulled back tightly. As I watched how she commanded the respect and the attention of the rest of the house slaves, I determined that her backbone was probably made from the toughest cedarwood.

Gaining her trust and agreement with the plan might not be as easy as I originally thought. Her loyalty to the master may be stronger than I hoped. On our fourth day there, as I noticed that the Baleines fully had the attention of the Remington's, I slipped into the kitchen as the house slaves worked to prepare.

When I entered, initially there were smiles on faces as people were in mid-conversation, but upon seeing me, they straightened, and Leona swiftly approached me. "Mr. Anderson, suh, is there anything you need?" she asked with the utmost tenderness and respect.

"Yes, ma'am," I said. My use of ma'am caused her brow to furrow in confusion. Me, a white man, refer to her, an old black woman, as ma'am? I noticed the looks on the faces of the other slaves as well. I touched Leona's hand tenderly and began to sing softly.

I've been in the storm so long.
I've been in the storm so long, children.
I've been in the storm so long.
Oh, give me little time to pray.

As I sang, I could sense all eyes on me in the stunned silence. Leona's eyes pierced mine and I saw her begin to closely examine my face and hair. Then her dark eyes began to water. When I finished, she placed her hand on my cheek, and I felt tears begin to roll down at the touch of a mother.

"Child, what are you doing out here with these white folks?" she said incredulously, as she quickly encircled me in a hug.

I chuckled. "They're friends," I said. I saw the look of alarm in her eyes and the others behind her. "They know," I said. "We've come to rescue you all."

"Rescue?" she asked.

"Set you free."

She had a little smirk on her face and put her hands on her hips. "And just how are you going to do that?"

I thought about how to say it, and then I noticed the expression on her face change. She then stepped forward again close to me and held my face in both of her hands.

"You listen to me, Mr. Anderson, or whatever your name is-"

"Azariah."

"Azariah," she said. "Don't you come to me for help with any ungodly ideas. I will not have it in my house!"

"Mama Leona," I said, giving her the respect I knew she was due. "They make you feel like this is your house, but it ain't. I bet you've seen people get sold off, whipped, and killed, maybe even experienced these things yourself." I walked over to the other ladies who still stood by watching me, enraptured. "My mama was once in Mama Leona's position, and she ain't never get anything from my master but misery. He sold off her husband and violated her. All my master ever gave me was suffering. I done lost my pa, my mama, my wife, and my daughter. Everyone and everything!" I felt hot tears burning, and I looked behind me to make sure the Remington's were still occupied and far away. "Why are you submitting to this evil? We are God's children!" I said passionately. "We are made in his image. We were not made for slavery! It is not his will!"

After allowing me to speak, Leona walked over to me swiftly, "You keep your voice down in here!" she said with great force. I pulled back and submitted to her. She spoke softly. "You right about many things, it is not His will for this evil to exist, but I do not submit to yo' plan. My faith is my way of saying, you c'n come this far, but no mo'. My master c'n never take this from me. If you think that killing them is going to be the answer, then you got the wrong woman to help you. I will not, and neither will any of my ladies. We will not sin against God to do His will."

We faced each other for a few moments

and then she held my hand again gently. "Do you not trust the Lord to care for us?"

Her still, small voice set off a shaking in my inner being. "I don't know." I answered honestly. At that moment, I wished that it was my mother standing before me, "Please let me save you," I said.

"Azariah," Leona said, "I am safe. Not from the Remingtons. I have enough sense to know better. But I'm safe in His arms. You must trust the Lord, or you'll truly have nothing left. He cares for you."

I felt the word escape my mouth before I had the chance to stop them. "No. He doesn't."

She squeezed my hand tighter and started to sing softly.

> *Somebody's knockin' at your door;*
> *Somebody's knockin' at your door;*
> *O sinner, why don't you answer?*
> *Somebody's knockin' at your door.*

She sang, *"Knocks like Jesus,"* and the ladies around her joined in. *"Somebody's knockin' at your door."* She sang again with more emotion, *"Knocks like Jesus."* Once again, the ladies responded, *"Somebody's knockin' at your door."* Then they all sang together, *"O sinner, why don't you answer? Somebody's knockin' at your door."*

> *Can't you hear him?*
> *Somebody's knockin' at your door.*
> *Can't you hear him?*
> *Somebody's knockin' at your door.*
>
> *O sinner, why don't you answer?*
> *Somebody's knockin' at your door.*
> *Jesus calls you,*
> *Somebody's knockin' at your door.*
> *Jesus calls you,*
> *Somebody's knockin' at your door.*
>
> *O sinner, why don't you answer?*
> *Somebody's knockin' at your door.*
> *Can't you trust him?*
> *Somebody's knockin' at your door.*
> *Can't you trust him?*

Somebody's knockin' at your door.
O sinner, why don't you answer?
Somebody's knockin' at your door.

Why did they want to stay here and suffer? Why did they not want my help? I bristled at the fact that it seemed implied that they thought that I was the one in need of true saving. That I needed to open my own heart to Jesus. In my frustration, I curtly replied, "Mama Leona, ladies, thank you for your song. I'll be on my way." I exited the kitchen.

***

Without the help of the kitchen staff, it had not been simple to figure out how to finish our plan. I spoke with Josephine and Caleb; we would have to skip the poison. Caleb wasn't sure about the change in plans, and offered that instead, we just move on to another plantation. But I felt that if Leona and the rest of the women were to just see that they could be free, that they would follow us North. So, we plotted for nighttime. In their sleep, Caleb and Josephine killed both Mr. and Mrs. Remington. I was assigned to handle their head overseer.

I snuck into his cabin, but right before I killed him, he woke, and he was quick at the draw, got his revolver and managed to shoot into my thigh. I got the bullet out and with great pain, I bandaged myself and put some honey in the wound to ward off infection. Caleb, Josephine and I worked on getting as many people as we could to leave with us. We just needed to get them across the border of Kentucky and Indiana. Seven of them came with us, but not the three women in the kitchen.

I stood by them stone-faced as we prepared to leave, "Are you so loyal to your master that you would stay even though he is dead?"

Mama Leona said, "Azariah, Master Remington was never my master. Mine is very much alive."

I felt the pain in my thigh quicken.

"Come," I pleaded. "You can be free like me."

She patted my hand, "I am freer than you are."

The two ladies with her looked at me with sadness, "Azariah, we will make sure to watch over her," one of them said.

"Go," the other said, "Get the others North before it's too late."

Leaving them behind was harder than I had imagined it would be. I did not truly know these women. They had questioned my salvation. I should have been content to leave them with their decision to remain enslaved. However, I found myself troubled each day and night on the journey home: troubled by their singing, troubled by Mama Leona's last words to me. We had a long journey home, and by the time I got there, I was desperately ill, my body feverish.

I lay on the floor, my body desperate for cool air. If the Lord had not sent me to Marshall's plantation none of this would have happened. I was happy here before he sent me.

Now, I was wishing that death would come sooner so I could find relief at last.

I heard the pitter patter of feet and as much I could, I propped myself up and dragged my body, so that I could use the wall to support myself. I took out my revolver and aimed, ready to shoot whoever appeared. I looked to see a man, but instead saw a small child, probably the age of five, coming from my bedroom. "Papa, I've been waiting here for you to come back home."

I stared, unable to believe who I was seeing. She was there, her curly hair roped into a braid, tiny wisps falling onto her face.

"Dovie?" I asked, groaning as I sat up.

"Papa, you look angry. Why are you angry?"

I wanted to tell her that I wasn't. But, even at five years old, Dove could always see through me. "Because I am hurt," I said, moving my hand to show her the blood covering my abdomen.

"How did you get hurt?"

I struggled for the words that would make

sense to her, that would pardon me. How could I tell her that her father was a murderer? "Remember when Vera had gotten in trouble, and they made us all go out there to see her get whipped? Remember how scared you were?" Honey and I had done our best to cover Dovie's face and keep her from seeing it, but she still had nightmares for days after.

"Yes, papa, I remember."

"Well, I went to fight someone like that, and I got him, but he also hurt me too."

She didn't say anything, but instead came over, sat beside me, and rested her head on my shoulder. "Why did you go there? I thought you told me that vengeance belongs to the Lord?"

"Sometimes God moves too slowly," I said gruffly.

When she faced me again, I noticed her eyes were bluer than I'd remembered them. Her eyes were like the strongest sea, the deepest river, or the clearest sky. "Or maybe you think that your justice is more righteous than our God. He told me he's gonna send someone else to do what you did not. She's family. She'll do it."

My body froze. "Don't be scared," she said to me tenderly. "Maybe God will heal you and you can come home and be with me and Mama."

It was then that I knew that I was not awake. *Was I dead already?*

"Where are you and Mama?"

She faced me, her eyes filled with excitement. "The best place! Grandma is here. Your pa is here too."

"Who else is there?" I asked, feeling winded. "Master Marshall is there. He's nice now." She got up and jumped up and down with glee. "And Jesus is there. He's the best. He takes walks with me all the time."

I clutched my wounded side and stared at her. "If I die, do you think I can be with you too?"

She seemed to freeze and then her face looked immediately dejected. "I asked him, and he said, you have to tell the truth first."

"Tell the truth about what."

She came close to me and placed her hand on my face. All at once, I saw Master Marshall in his last moments, his body mutilated, and dozens of souls, who once would never have believed this man could show an ounce of compassion towards the slave, watched him sacrificing his life in the name of one. I felt compassion for the first time as I realized why Reeves and Marshall had never given us the gospel. They had never really understood it themselves. They gave us a gospel of greed because that's what had been passed on to them. I saw Paul ordering the death of Stephen. I saw Paul on the road to Damascus. I saw Paul preaching and writing. I saw Paul beheaded. The punishment for the murder of Stephen and others should have been death and Paul did die. But God had shown him the grace of salvation and he in turn brought others to salvation, even though he would not escape his end.

I saw myself. The lives I had cut short. The lies I'd told.

For once I understood the justice of God,

the patience of God, and the love of God in a way I had never understood before. He spoke to me kindly, even though I did not deserve it. "Azariah, you have reasons to be angry. But, is it right for you to be angry?"

I opened my mouth to answer, but I felt such shame that no words came.

Naima

PENNSYLVANIA

1845-1859

Woe.

To understand my story, you must understand how that one word changed everything for me. I remember waking up in a pool of sweat hearing that one word resonating deep within me. I was born in 1841, and I wasn't much older than seven years when the dreams started. The first one was of a house with white pillars, its pillars appeared as candles that melted down to the ground. Later that evening, as my family sat with the gang and everyone spoke freely about the next set of runaways they were bound to help capture, that I heard the rest of the message.

Woe to them that devise iniquity, and work evil upon their beds! when the morning is light, they practice it, because it is in the power of their hand. And they covet fields, and take them by violence; and houses, and take them away: so they oppress a man and his house, even a man and his heritage. Therefore thus saith the LORD; Behold, against this family do I devise an evil, from which ye shall not remove your necks; neither shall ye go haughtily: for this time is evil.

I was born as a free woman. I had never known the weight of bondage, the sting of a whip, or the pain of having loved ones sold away. But my mama and daddy had. Their backs still bear the scars. My daddy's fingers are still damaged from the years of picking cotton and my mama worked in the house, but she didn't like to talk about it much. Papa used to tell me a story that his mother and his mother's mother used to tell her. The Fante sold the Asante for guns and vice versa. Everyone must look out for their tribe.

For my father and mother, our tribe had always been merely our household. The rest of the people on their respective plantations were also just people willing to look out for themselves if need be. "If a man had to choose between his wife being sold or you being sold, he's picking you," my father would say. "So, I look out for me and mine."

My parents didn't initially love each other. They had been chosen for each other. My father was a troublemaker, they had said. He had been sold from a former owner and already had many lashes on his back. They wanted him to marry someone they felt would keep him tame. My father had been a prisoner of war during tribal warfare back in his homeland, and he said that one day after his capture, he had woken in this terrible castle dungeon and was taken to a boat that was far worse than anything he could've imagined. He'd told me that human suffering looked like watching men have their jaws broken as they were force fed and watching women dragged beneath the deck to be raped. To endure a ship that smelled like urine, feces, and vomit, all of it falling on you as the boat tossed and turned. It sounded like unanswered groans, prayers, and tears. When he emerged from that trek alive, he said that he was determined to live life on his own terms. Initially this meant disobeying orders, but eventually he said that he had begun to realize the wisest way was to learn the language of the white man and then plot his escape. He had been taken to Brazil first and then to the Caribbean, and then eventually smuggled to America via Charleston. He said that he had been sold on the Charleston market to the Marshall Plantation in Tennessee. His new master heard that he could be trouble, but he was a big man and good for work. He was immediately ordered to marry. His master thought this would soften his stubbornness.

When he was told to marry my mother, they seemed to be at odds about everything until they realized they had two things in common: a desire for freedom and a desire to not bring any more children into this world as slaves. Shortly after they were married, they began to plot their escape, and they did. They successfully got from Tennessee to Ohio and lived free for about seven years. During this time, they ended up getting pregnant with a boy who died in childbirth. My mother doesn't like to talk about him much. My father told me that my mother had thought that it was a punishment from God that she had lost him, a life for a life. I didn't understand what that meant at the time. Although, they hadn't planned to have another child, they ended up with me.

Their free life in Ohio was bliss. My father finally got his dream of living life on his own terms again. What they didn't account for was that once caught, they would be forced to join a gang that worked on capturing other runaways. The gang forced our little family to leave Ohio and travel on the road with them. We were initially forced to work as bait for these runaways, gaining their trust and then luring them to the hook of capture and return to captivity. But my parents were never keen on remaining enslaved, whether it was on a plantation or in a chain gang. I distinctly remember hearing them plan and plot how they would get out of this. I remember covering my ears as they shot and killed every person in that chain gang one night as they slept. They took back their fake manumission papers and I thought that would be that.

My parents had been carefully watching this chain gang during the time they had been enslaved by them and now they meant to keep the business going, and they would lead it. It made a good influx of money, so much so that they betrayed their own experiences, their own brothers and sisters, by luring and capturing people and transporting them South. They hated slavery, but they loved money more. They didn't just want have freedom; they wanted wealth too.

But by the time I turned 15, the passage of the Fugitive Slave Act came. This empowered men to come in from slave states to shackle anyone's newfound freedom. My parents went from just capturing runaways to abducting anyone who was Black (born free or not) and transporting them to the South for a cut of the reward money. With the money they had amassed, they were finally able to do the things they had always dreamed of doing: they finally had their own land and home (even if was technically stolen from a free man that they had abducted and sent down South). They were able to purchase their own free papers and now with the security of a home in Pennsylvania, they carefully selected a place to live. It was the ideal location due to all the slaves trying to escape to Philadelphia and the fact that Pennsylvania bordered West Virginia, which still practiced slavery. Not to mention they began to have an influx of money. They finally had the family life they wanted. My father told me that he had named me Naima, because I was his comfort, and he wanted to finally give me the life that I deserved.

Instead, I became the daughter who wrecked their life with one word.

Woe.

***

Once we left the chain gang and moved to Pennsylvania, the cloud of fear that hung over us seemed to have melted away. Our needs were always met. We had food, a lovely home, we had each other. My parents were loving and attentive. In fact, it seemed to make no sense that my mother and father surrounded me with God's Word after everything that had transpired and everything they were currently doing. They encouraged me to read the Word and learn it. I think they did because although they did not follow any of God's ways, they knew what it was like to be restricted from reading, and the Bible was the easiest book to obtain, so they let me read it as much as I wanted to. We prayed together at the dinner table and at nights all together. But now, I understand that while the words I read every day became life to me, it had always just been nice platitudes to my parents.

My parents knew all the information about God's nature, his holiness, his goodness, his kindness, his justice, his peace without ever experiencing it.

There are still moments when I wrestle with feelings of guilt, that I ruined the seemingly perfect life that we once had. But I know that a life built on sin, no matter how good it may appear, is rotten on the inside. Our home, a beautiful colonial style home with large columns and a sweeping entryway, reminded me of the house in my dream and I often waited day after day for the house to melt away.

We wrestled with termites that ate away at the foundation of our home, and no matter how my mother had our servants Patrick and Sabrina clean, the candles would always burn too quickly, the dust would run into our home as quickly as it was swept out, and a moldy smell would reappear. My parents were whitewashed sepulchers. They looked like the perfect law-abiding freemen. We went to church, we gave to our community and at night is when they would be their true selves. All the things we did during the day were to insulate the community around us from knowing what really happened at night. Their allowance of my love for the Bible was merely to help them keep up their act.

My parents would blame Patrick and Sabrina for our house and threaten to sell them back to their former masters. You see, Patrick and Sabrina had been a husband-and-wife runaway, and instead of returning them back to their master for money, my parents kept them as their own slaves. They felt like they were doing some good in the world because at least they didn't beat them, but Patrick and Sabrina lived in fear every day.

When I first started to hear the voice of the Lord, it would always come to me in my dreams. I don't know how to explain my dreams. They did not fill me with terror. They seemed to come from the Holy Spirit himself, allowing me to…feel. I felt what others felt as they were being taken away from their families and sold into slavery. I would hear chains, feel the weight of someone holding me down. I would wake up screaming for my parents, scared that I was being carried away just like I had seen the others carried away. But whenever I woke and came to, it was not fear and terror, it was grief. I felt how grieved the Holy Spirit was, and it drove me into prayer and when I got older, into fasting. I prayed for those souls we returned back to terror or even death. I didn't have much of a choice. My parents would not even let me get too close to whomever they captured, for fear that they would hurt me in retribution, but I knew the Lord heard my prayers.

I knew what my parents did for money. They never hid it from me. They felt like it would be much more work to hide it than it would be to just let me see and eventually learn the trade myself. Sometimes they would make me a part of their bait. Who more would you trust than your fellow black man who also had a little girl?

My mother had fair skin and light brown curly hair and could pass as a white woman, and so she constantly went back and forth, choosing a different identity based on who she was trying to bait. When she was trying to gain a runaway or a freeman's trust so she could capture and sell them, she was married to my father, and I was her sweet little brown child, a combination of both of their skin tones. I looked like our mother, so when she posed a white woman, I had to stay away. My father acted as her coach driver, and she would mix with wealthy company and find out information that would lead to more money.

At first, when I started having these dreams, my parents took pity on me. Poor Naima, she has nightmares of being taken away. They would hold me tight and assure me that everything was ok. But then I started dreaming about a young teenager, her golden-brown skin illuminated by the sun. She hummed to herself in a field filled with yellow and purple wildflowers before being overpowered by an older white man. Something so vile happening in such a beautiful place. That same young lady with a large belly heading back to the field in anguish, giving birth. I was so young that the dream didn't even make much sense to me. I had no concept of what rape even was at this time.

When I was younger, my mama and I used to go outside and hang up clothes on the clothesline. She never had Sabrina do it, unless she was too busy or ill to do it herself. She said that it was the one thing that relaxed her. "Mama," I said. "Have you ever heard God speak to you?"

"No, Naima, I've never heard God speak to me," she said, applying a clothespin to the line.

"I think God speaks to me," I said.

She paused, "What does he say to you?"

I told her about my dream. She dropped her pins as she whispered to herself, "That's why she named me Meadow."

I had always known my mother's name to be Georgia Mae, amongst the many other aliases she used whenever we were on the road. I never understood what she meant until much later. She had collected herself from the shock of hearing about my dream and then said to me, "God doesn't concern himself with us."

"But I thought that God loves us. That's what they said in church."

"Yes, there's what they say in church and there's the way things just are. God has other things to do in this world, I suppose. He doesn't concern himself with us. We just do our best to make sure that we take care of ourselves."

"Then why did Jesus die for us if he doesn't care about us?"

She stopped working and knelt to be eye level with me. Speaking gently to me, she said. "God, Jesus, the Holy Spirit, they're things that just make people feel better. Life is hard, people suffer, and if God cared, then we wouldn't. People just comfort themselves with Jesus. Do you understand?"

I nodded. I understood then that my mother did not know Jesus. From then on, it was my personal mission at night to pray for my mother's conversion. I would even tell people at church to keep the secret that I think my mom needs Jesus and to join me in prayer. One sweet older lady, Mrs. Burns did help me pray.

I had my next set of visions, one of a young girl, her skin so light that she could be mistaken for a white child, playing with another young girl in the home. They grew older and were no longer playmates, one served the other, even though they looked very much alike. The servant girl and the other girl became women, and both married tall men they smiled at. But the mistress' husband covered the servant's mouth as she screamed and cried. The servant girl tried to tell her mistress, but then she was sent away. The servant girl looked exactly like my mother.

Mama had woken me up that morning, and as soon as I saw her face, I rose up and hugged her. "Mama, I'm so sorry that happened to you. Are you ok?" She was very confused, but when I told my mother, her eyes grew wide. "It ain't God telling you these things. It's the devil. The devil tryna remind me of things that should be forgotten."

None of these things made sense to me. I used to rehearse the visions to myself so that I wouldn't forget them, and when I hit my teenage years, I began to write the visions down. When I was older, I was finally able to understand that my mother had been the baby born in the field, a baby born out of suffering, a child with skin so white and made to serve her biological sister, a young woman who had carved out some happiness in life with my father, but then she was violated by her sister's husband. After she'd gone to her sister, who she thought she could trust for protection, her sister out of anger and jealousy, had plotted to sel her away from her husband. That's what made my mother run. The visions continued, the messages of woe continued, and the more I received them, the more I was filled with dread for my parents and prayed for their salvation. By the time I was sixteen, I had books and books of prayers, written petitions for my parents to finally see and know the Lord.

In the final vision, I remember having it come to a head when I realized how my mother had truly escaped from her plantation. In my dream I saw that she paid a man she called Aaron to take her far away and then they heard people coming and she left him and then tore at her clothes and then screamed and when white men came to her rescue, she said, "That ape tried to rape me. He took me out here and tried to rape me!" She claimed that she hadn't seen his face, but that he'd knocked her out and taken her out here and when she came to, she'd fought him off and screamed.

Her story didn't make much sense. But it didn't need to. For the next few days and nights, the nearby townsmen hunted down black men while my mother, who had also devised a plan for my father's escape, met up with him, and then disappeared. Now, I understood: a life for a life.

From that dream I remember that my father had to shake me awake from the terror of what I witnessed those men and their families experience. In one of my visions, I saw my mother and father on trial, I saw the judge's gavel strike downwards with force. I felt their guilt, I felt the weight of their sentence as the courtroom, and the beautiful home and the world my parents had fashioned with their own hand, melted like wax around me. I felt the heat of the flames. My mother and father stood in the doorway as I sat up in the darkness and said to them what I heard in my dream.

"Therefore thus saith the Lord; Behold, against this family do I devise an evil, from which ye shall not remove your necks; neither shall ye go haughtily: for this time is evil. In that day shall one take up a parable against you, and lament with a doleful lamentation, and say, We be utterly spoiled: he hath changed the portion of my people: how hath he removed it from me! turning away he hath divided our fields."

My parents rebuked me harshly. These things could never happen to them. The only people who really needed to be punished for the sins of the nation were still flourishing. God must be patient to deal with them and more so with us. My mother tried to beat me into submission, but to no avail. The visions did not stop, and the messages kept coming, sometimes I would talk in my sleep. My mother considered sending me out of the house. I still did not relent; I felt like judgment was imminent and that their repentance was a life-or-death situation. I tried to tell them about who God is, his nature, but no matter what I said, the reasons for their sins remained the same: where was God when they were suffering under the hands of Master Marshall and their masters before him? Why couldn't it be their turn to have something? No, to have everything that had been taken from them?

They said that their only curse was being born into this world that was cruel to them and that their only child had resorted to cursing them instead of being thankful for all that they had given me, even if it had come at the price of others' lives. They claimed that I would never understand what they had to do to survive and thrive in this world because I had never known slavery. I told them if I had known it, I would never be able to inflict that suffering on another. When I turned 18, I questioned whether to leave their home, because I feared being swept away with their looming judgment. I did not know when, but I knew that it would come when they least expected it.

When I turned eighteen, my visions were no longer mostly of my mother, but now of my father. I saw our father as a young boy. I saw him weeping over the body of a mutilated man. When I asked him about it for the first time, I saw him filled with uncontrollable rage. Like it had been stored up and bridled this whole time and now was ready to be let loose.

He began to curse and flung a chair against the wall until it broke, sending splinters everywhere. When he calmed down, he explained how his father had died in a battle between two tribes back at his home. His father had been the leader and instead of being killed, they had sold him to the white men.

He no longer wanted to hear my "chatter" about who God is. I tried talking about his love. I tried talking about his holiness. I tried talking about his goodness. I grew discouraged and knew that all I could do moving forward was pray that God would continue to be patient with them.

I did not want these dreams anymore. What I wanted more than anything was for God to just hold his hand, hold back his wrath. But sometimes I felt like I could feel the weight of the prayers of everyone that had been enslaved begging for justice. It was like I was trying to keep a closet door closed when the mess behind the door was piling up and straining against the hinges. I wanted justice for the enslaved too, but I knew that while justice for them meant the consumption of those who had hurt my parents, it also meant judgment for my parents as well. I needed more time for them to truly see.

God had been patient with them. I wanted him to just hold on a little while longer, but could I truly blame him if he did not?

I'll never forget that I was eighteen and it was October 1st, the day that we were sitting around the dining table enjoying Sabrina's roasted chicken and vegetables when suddenly there was a knock at the door. Sabrina went to answer it and before I knew it at least six men rushed into our dining room, guns in hand, four of them pointed at my father, and one at my mother and one pointed at me. Fear permeated my entire body. I felt like I was swimming and then drowning in it as I heard the words, "runaway". I had been at the opposite end of this to know what would be coming next.

He was slow to anger and great in power, but just as he said, he will not at all acquit the wicked.

Naima

TENNESSEE

1859-1870

I wiped at her forehead, her skin red, hot to the touch. Mrs. Caroline Babel hadn't eaten much in weeks and had wasted away, her body too frail to get out of bed, so her once luxurious red hair lay greasy and limp on her pillow. She was in her 50s, much older than my 29 years, yet lying on her pillow, she looked completely elderly, with her cheeks and eyes sunken. She only had the strength to let off a terrible cough and then sink back into bed, exhausted and defeated. Mrs. Caroline was known for her riveting speeches to women to remember the fallen soldiers of the Confederacy. I have attended some of these speeches as her servant. I watched as her burned hands waved with fervor as she spoke like any preacher. Polished women with their hair curled and coiffed under beautiful hats, their dresses with their elaborate details speaking of their wealth, sat spellbound by her. Even women who didn't have much, their dresses looking a tad worn, still pulled out their best to attend these events. They had started to make great gains to change the minds of those who had felt defeated, depressed and displaced after the war.

The war had never been about slavery, but instead the states' rights to protect their agricultural way of life. The North had only won because it had more wealth, but the South was the one with the moral footing, they still believed that this was God's country instead of those godless Yankees who had come in and left the women to suffer after killing their husbands in war. Slaves had always been family members that were willing workers and had done their part to willingly fight alongside the Confederacy. The memories of these fallen soldiers needed to be protected and memorialized. Well, not the former slaves who had fought. Just the white Confederate soldiers.

Forgive me if I seem a bit sarcastic. It's only now that I can share my true feelings. For all these years as a slave and then as Miss Caroline's maid, which was a minor upgrade to enslavement, I had to bite my tongue and assure her of her brilliance. Until I had her on her deathbed. When she began to show signs of consumption, at no point did she ever express concern that I may also become sick, especially when it began to spread throughout the house. Her husband died first. I suspect she didn't mind that, they seemed to hate one another. But then, her only son passed as well, and since then, she seemed to just accept death's looming presence. Once she was so delirious with fever that she accused me of doing this to her. I must be a witch because I hadn't gotten sick myself. Not a cough or sniffle. I could not explain to her why. I did not know why myself.

"Light that candle over there for me," Mrs. Caroline ordered me to the melted stub of a candle left on the golden candlestick. Dusk was fast approaching.

"There isn't much wax left on this one, Mrs. Caroline. I can grab a fresh one for you," I said.

"No need to waste any more candles, this one will have to do," she said. "Give me words of comfort, Naima," she commanded.

"What would you like me to tell you, Mrs. Caroline?" I said looking quickly into her green eyes and then away. I obliged her, as usual.

"Perhaps a verse or two from the Bible. Read them to me."

I did not know what to say to her. I just opened the Bible and looked down. I saw the verse and knew that I should read it because it was true, but that I shouldn't because it was not the truth that she wanted. But if this woman were to pass from Earth into eternity today, she might as well hear the truth rather than lovely platitudes.

So, I read, "*Blessed is he whose transgression is forgiven, whose sin is covered. Blessed is the man unto whom the Lord imputeth not iniquity, and in whose spirit there is no guile. When I kept silence, my bones waxed old through my roaring all the day long. For day and night thy hand was heavy upon me: my moisture is turned into the drought of summer. Selah. I acknowledge my sin unto thee, and mine iniquity have I not hid. I said, I will confess my transgressions unto the Lord; and thou forgavest the iniquity of my sin. Selah. For this shall every one that is godly pray unto thee in a time when thou mayest be found: surely in the floods of great waters they shall not come nigh unto him. Thou art my hiding place; thou shalt preserve me from trouble; thou shalt compass me about with songs of deliverance. Selah. I will instruct thee and teach thee in the way which thou shalt go: I will guide thee with mine eye. Be ye not as the horse, or as the mule, which have no understanding: whose mouth must be held in with bit and bridle, lest they come near unto thee. Many sorrows shall be to the wicked: but he that trusteth in the Lord, mercy shall compass him about. Be glad in the Lord, and rejoice, ye righteous: and shout for joy, all ye that are upright in heart."*

She sat quietly and listened to the whole psalm, and then said sharply, "Why did you read that to me?"

"David wrote this psalm. For as long as his sins were unconfessed, his body felt consumed." I swallowed hard, knowing that the time had come. She was on her deathbed; I had to do it now. I had long avoided doing what the Lord had asked me to do when he instructed me to not escape for my freedom North and to stay in the South, knowing that I would be forced to work for someone who had once owned slaves. I had raged against the Lord. I had been angry with him for a long time, that he had allowed me to see the end of legalized slavery, but he was denying me freedom with his command that I stay here, and now with her, of all people. Mrs. Caroline and her husband had been friends of my former master. They had just moved down to the South right before that day of judgment had come. They were greeted warmly by Master

Marshall and invited to spend some time at the big house until they finished building their own house.

They attended parties with Master Marshall, and it was at one of those parties that I knew Mrs. Caroline had burned her hands even though she often told others in her speeches that her hands had been burned by Union soldiers. I doubt she realized that I knew the story behind the burned flesh on her hands. I was just another black face in the crowd serving food that night.

For a while, I knew the word that he wanted me to tell Miss Caroline, but no time had ever seemed like the right time. Especially after all I had already suffered. Speaking this word at the wrong time could have me one day surrounded by white hoods and a rope. But, as I looked at her lying in bed, her eyes sinking into her head, her lips pale, I said, "Mrs. Caroline, the spirit of man is the candle of the Lord, searching all the inward parts of the belly."

Her eyes snapped to mine, with a flash of anger. "How did you know the inscription on the candlestick?"

The inscription? I had never even come close enough to truly notice. She saw the confusion on my face. "How…did…you-"

I didn't know how to explain, so I continued, "The Lord… he speaks to me…You must tell the truth about the War between the States and the life that existed before then. The life that still exists now."

She looked fearful, and then she narrowed her eyes on me. "Charles warned me about you."

At the mention of him, I felt a chill go down my spine. She never talked about him. "What did he warn you about?

"He told me you were just like that other liar. Azariah. The one that nearly ruined the family. But, I did not believe that some black gal could be responsible. People say you have powers."

Of course they would say this about me. Rather than address their own sin and acknowledge God, they would of course resort to the notion that I must be a witch. My chuckle was laced with annoyance. "I have no magical powers. Only the power given to me through God's Holy Spirit. I did not bring destruction to the Marshall Plantation. God did. I merely was sent to bring a message, just as I am bringing a message to you now."

"Am I going to die?" she asked.

"If you are asking me if you will die now, then I will say, I don't know. But if you are asking me if you will eventually die, then the answer is yes. As we all will."

She scowled at me with annoyance. "I will not be like my foolish brother. Go ahead and speak your message."

"Come into agreement with God about your sin and repent."

"What sin?" she said blisteringly. "You want me to believe that our way of life is sinful? That the North is much better?"

"It is. We live in freedom there."

"Freedom," she scoffed. "Your people live in an illusion of freedom in North. Believe it or not, I lived there. My husband and I went there thinking that we might make some money there and it was all for nothing."

"Why did you come back?"

She thought for a moment and then looked at me coldly. "In the North, it was just hypocrisy. They claimed that they cared about the rights of blacks. They only cared about looking self-righteous." She started to cough, and I gave her some water. She continued. "They still believed and treated you as you were, subhuman. They only thought they were better because they didn't put you to work like we did. So, I came back home. I missed my family. I missed Tennessee, and these Yankees came and ruined my home."

I understood what she meant about the North. Those of us who still inhabited our bodies, encased in our dark skin, knew all too well that we could not escape the discrimination we faced wherever we went. But, I knew that she also used this as a shield to help her reconcile and justify her own sin.

"The lies you tell others about the war have only been to fortify you from the lies that you tell yourself."

"You little witch, I have not told any lies about the war, about anything!"

"Mrs. Caroline, you have told your story. But have you ever stopped to ask the story of a slave? Have you ever thought not just about your life being turned upside down by the war, but of the slave whose life was forever impacted by servitude, by rape, by separation from family, by violence?"

She stared at me for a moment and considered this. Maybe it was her sick state that made her even willing to listen to my words. Maybe The Spirit himself was opening her heart. Whatever her motivation, I heard her say with a hint of annoyance and perhaps some curiosity, "Tell me yours."

***

I was eighteen years old when I was

brought to Red Oaks. It was October 1859. My parents did not like to talk much about Red Oaks. There was only one story I've heard them tell. They once joked about how foolish the Marshalls were for keeping some candlestick encased and protected because they thought it brought them good luck. Even I had laughed along.

I remember thinking that it was a beautiful property with its big white house and trees all around. We arrived in the autumn, so I understood why it was called Red Oaks, because the trees truly did set the stage. But there was also something terrifying in those trees as well. The trees made the house look like it was on fire, and I asked myself if it was possible that just like sin could look attractive on the outside, but be horrible on the inside, if this place that looked beautiful to the naked eye, could really just be hell in disguise.

As a part of the Fugitive Slave Act, my mother and father had to be returned to their previous owner. I had no previous owner, but the justification was that Marshall owned my mother and therefore owned me. My mother's former master was no longer alive, and his son now ran the plantation. I heard that his father had been a brutal master, quick to whip or even kill, and that he had sired many babies. There was something else about him that people would not tell me. They told me that if the current master heard them discussing it, they would be punished.

When we were being transported to Red Oaks, I was filled with panic from the unknown. My parents instead were filled with terror from what they knew they would face. When they were brought here, both were branded on their cheeks as runaways and beaten within an inch of their lives.

The master took pity on me. He decided not to brand nor beat me. I was sent to the house to work. When you work in the house, I realized, you learn many things about the history of the family and how the family runs. I was told that he once had a wife, but that he had treated her with cold indifference. The women on the plantation told me that just like his father, Master Marshall preferred his slave women to his wife. His wife then started up an affair with another man, and when it was discovered, her husband had beaten her badly. She had been with child and had lost her pregnancy. She and her lover had been planning to run away together. But now that she had been found out and had lost her child, her grief had consumed her, and she hung herself. To his social circles he told them that she had been struggling with grief after having a miscarriage. He would even weep and played the perfect role as the grieving widow. He made it known that he was planning on not remarrying again after such a loss. But to everyone on the plantation, he presented the truth. He did not remarry because he did not feel the need to. Not when he had access to all of us.

Master Marshall immediately selected me to remain close to him. I would recoil just from the sight of his golden blond hair that he merely slicked back so that he would look somewhat presentable with his scruffy beard. Before we had been enslaved, my mother had warned me that if a woman's master wanted this, then she was doomed. The first time he came to my quarters, as he approached me, the word from the Lord tumbled out of my mouth before I could even think about taking the words back.

And the Lord hath given a commandment concerning thee, that no more of thy name be sown: out of the house of thy gods will I cut off the graven image and the molten image: I will make thy grave; for thou art vile.

He looked merely amused by what I said. I think he just thought that I was crazy. He approached me silently and as I retreated, he only laughed, knowing my efforts to get away would be futile, and continued his evil.

✳✳✳

In the house there were portraits of his late mother, whom he often referred to lovingly. The women in the house told me she was extremely demanding and hardly ever satisfied. If she commanded a woman to be whipped, her son made sure to see that it was done.

An older woman named Chloe seemed to oversee the rest of the women and men who worked in the house. Master Marshall seemed to trust that she would ensure that everything in the house stayed to his liking. She had dark leathery skin, but the softest and tenderest touch and voice. She was well liked and mostly just hummed hymns as she cleaned. Whenever my duties in the house were complete, she would encourage me to check on how my parents were recovering. I would pray over them, but my mother never spoke to me. My father instead raged at my prayers, telling me that those prayers were useless.

Once they recovered and my mama was sent back to work in the fields, I made it my duty to sneak away to check on her. It was easy to tell that many of the older people here did not like her. At first, I could not understand why, and then I remembered my dream. How my mother left this plantation was a complete betrayal. She had cost men their lives.

She was still not speaking a word to me, but at least she was still here with me. Until the day she was not. I felt my heart beating out of my chest as I searched for her. I searched her cabin and all around, and then I remembered the field, the meadow from my dream and ran as fast as I could there. There she was, lying in the grass, her wrists bleeding out in a field about a mile away from the plantation. A rusty scrap of metal lay nearby.

As she bled out, I remembered holding her wrists tightly to stop the bleeding and begging her to repeat after me as I said, "Lord, forgive me for my sins." She only looked at me, delirious, and still silently defiant. I tried to stop the bleeding. I kept telling her how much I loved her while screaming for help. All I wanted her to say in those moments were those words of repentance. But they never came out of her mouth. She wouldn't even mouth them, and it broke me.

All I wanted to do was save her.

***

My grief was thick. Why had the Lord not answered our prayers? Why had he brought me here? I dreaded having to tell my father about what happened to my mother. The day after I told him, during his work in the fields, my father grabbed the overseer off his horse, took a rock, and bludgeoned him to death in front of everyone. He was shot immediately to keep from attacking anyone else. I was in the house when it happened.

For days afterward, my father's mutilated body dangled above us as a warning to the rest of us. I was never allowed to publicly mourn him. Master Marshall watched closely to make sure that I did not. He demanded my loyalty in that way, especially since he was the only one holding me back from being attacked and killed by the rest of the overseers. I knew my father felt like he had finally managed to get some sort of revenge. He had experienced life as a free man and he had also killed one of his enslavers. Even though he and my mother made life increasingly more difficult for me after their deaths, I did not blame them. I saw them as lost souls.

I focused my anger on God. I could not understand why he didn't give them more time. If they had more time then they may have had a chance to change. He had been the one to bring us to this God-forsaken plantation. But then one night, I heard singing.

Rock of ages cleft for me
Let me hide myself in Thee
Rock of ages, cleft for me
Let me hide myself in Thee

I followed the sound of the music and found myself deep in the woods. As I approached, I saw an old woman, broken and weathered by years of hard work. Mrs. Chloe. As she and about five others sang in the dark of the woods, with just the faint moonlight peeking in through the trees, she looked to me to be so serenely whole. Everyone turned to look at me.

None stopped singing and she motioned for me to come join them.

> *Let the water and the blood*
> *From thy riven side which flowed*
> *Oh, be of sin the double cure*
> *Cleanse me from its guilt and power*

I stood with them, but I did not have the strength to sing with them. To sing right now would be a lie, because I felt betrayed by the God that I had served and trusted. She held out her hand towards me, I walked to her, and she held me in an embrace.

> *Nothing in my hand I bring*
> *Simply to Thy cross I cling*
> *Nothing in my hand I bring*
> *Simply to Thy cross I cling*

She finally spoke to me. "It's ok to mourn what was, what is, and what will never be."

***

From that day on, I lived in Chloe's home now that I was officially an orphan. Time moved

247

slowly in that place, and I struggled to remember the month and year. It might have been grief or just survival, but the days just seemed hazy. I was with Chloe for at least half a year before everything changed. Chloe knew my mother from the day she had been born until the day she had left the plantation. She knew my grandmother, she told me all she could about her. Her kindness. Her strength and how she had cared for so many on this plantation. She told me about her late husband George and how she was grateful that he got to die peacefully in his sleep. She even told me she knew my uncle, but my mother had never mentioned having a brother.

"How have you survived this long at this place?"

She laughed. "I was born on this plantation. My parents belonged to Master Marshall's grandfather. My grandparents belonged to the Marshall before that. They were his first slaves. Chile, it's only the grace of God."

Generations trapped in this. "Have you ever thought about what life would've been like outside of this place?"

She sighed, "Yes, there were many nights that George and I dreamed of that. Many days that I still feel guilty that I was too scared to seize the chance to be free."

"You had a chance to run away?"

"No, I had the chance to be free."

"I don't understand."

"Many years ago, we had somethin' strange happen here. Back then it was the elder Master Marshall, his name was Arthur Marshall, and his son now is Charles Marshall. The farm over yonder was Master Reeves. They chose a young boy to be the preacher over here. His name was Azariah. Handsome boy, his skin was so light, he could pass for white. But as he grew, he started really teaching us the Bible, and they punished him by selling his daddy, and then by whipping him. He stopped preaching out in the open so much. He kinda stuck to what they wanted him to say for a bit. He even got him a wife and child. Honey and Dove." She looked away for a moment. "I miss them. Dove was with me and with Meadow and Little Miss Marshall."

"You were with my mother?"

"I was Little Miss Marshall's helper. Meadow was her companion. Dove was assigned to the house and keeping her with me or with her grandmother was the only way to keep her safe."

"What happened to Dove?"

"Her mother Honey picked up and ran to her freedom one day and never returned. She took Dove with her."

"Without her husband?"

"Yes. It almost broke Azariah." She sighed. "Then one day Azariah ran away. No one saw him for some years, and then one night, he just appeared right here in this cabin. I couldn't believe my eyes. He told us that he came back to tell Master Marshall a message from the Lord, and I just thought that this man was crazy. Your uncle-"

"My uncle?"

"Azariah."

"My mother never mentioned him."

"He left when she was young. I reckon she never knew he was her brother. Master Marshall was both of their fathers."

A sick churning began in my stomach, and I dropped my head in my hands. "So, the current Master is my-"

"Uncle."

I felt like I was going to be sick. Chloe held my hand. "I'm sorry, Naima."

"Does every form of evil exist in this place?"

"Yes," she said sadly.

"God is not in this place."

She squeezed my hand. "Yes, he is. Right here with you and me and with anyone else who believes in his name." She took her hand and cupped my cheek. "When your uncle came, what seemed impossible, became possible. Master Marshall and Master Reeves got down on their knees and repented. Little Miss Marshall even fasted and prayed to the Lord. She left to the North. But his wife and son remained as hard-hearted as ever. Your mother had left by this time, she never got to see what happened here. But they freed everyone on this plantation, they offered each of us passage to the North or full wages for our labor."

"What?"

"God did answer. God does answer."

"Why didn't you leave?"

"To be honest, I was too scared. I didn't know if he would change his mind. I didn't know if he was plottin' against us. George wanted to go and we got ready to go, but I stopped to pray about it and I felt that I needed to stay."

"You gave up your opportunity?!"

"Yes, the Lord had shown me someone to come, and I needed to be here for them. So, I stayed and helped his wife, she had never let go of her feelings about us, but I had hopes that maybe when Master Marshall came back, that everything would be ok, that those of us left behind would receive the wages that we were promised. But when Master Marshall left, he was killed."

"What happened to his daughter? The one

that you took care of?”

"She was young miss when all of this happened. I think she resented that her mother had not moved them up North like her father had suggested. When her father died, she was lost. She was more attached to him than her mother. But she had both of them in her. She would try to be nice to us, maybe try to talk them out of whippin’ one of us. But she…she still didn’t want us to touch her. She still looked at us like we were nothing better than horse dung outside. Then when things happened with Meadow…”

“Mrs. Chloe, all this time and you haven’t told me any of this.”

“You wasn’t ready for this.”

“What makes you think I’m ready now?”

“Because God sent you. He showed it to me a long time ago. You the woman to come and bring the Lord’s judgment to this place. You the woman I gave up freedom for.”

Her words made me pause. Her eyes were fixed on me. “Judgment?” I said in disbelief.

"I'm not bringing any more words of judgment. All it's ever brought is misery."

"Any more?"

I tried to keep my tears at bay. "It's my fault they're not here."

She held my hands firmly. "Your parents…" Then she lifted my chin. "You only responsible to bring the Word, not to make people follow it."

I wiped at my face. "Why did God make me like this? I don't want these dreams. I don't want these words."

"What do you want?"

No one had ever asked me that. I thought about it. "I want…I want for all the cruelty to stop."

"That's why you're the right person. You don't want revenge. You want justice and how you suppose for God to end it? With a flood? He already done did that. He even sent his son. What's left when we won't even believe in Jesus and repent?"

I rubbed my forehead.

She continued. "Judgment ain't always a bad thing you know. If God don't show that he mad about evil, then how do we know that he's really good and holy? Naima, judgment is only the first part. Sometimes things have to burn in order for buds to grow. Gold must be burned to be molded into something new."

"What did God show you? How will I do this?"

"I don't think I should tell you details. But just know he's going to use you, and this plantation will be no more. Forever."

***

"A month later, after this, is when I first met you Mrs. Caroline. We were in the house, Chloe and I, and I often had to help her do chores because she was getting older and couldn't manage as well. We were washing dishes; I was washing, and she was drying. Olive let you and your husband in the house and when she saw you-"

"She dropped the plate," Mrs. Caroline said. It was the only time she had stopped me to say anything.

I nodded. "Yes." I felt like my body was trembling with a mix of rage, sadness, and sickness.

Mrs. Caroline looked even more feeble in her bed now staring up at me. "She knew who I was," she said softly.

I nodded again. "Yes, she did."

I saw her eyes become glassy. "I have been listening to you for a long time now. I need rest. Please leave."

I thought about ignoring her, considering that she was helpless and the only person here taking care of her was me. She had no choice but to sit and listen to me tell her every detail. But instead, I just nodded, leaving the candle burning next to her and walking away.

***

It was nearly midnight when I heard her

voice calling for me again. It was weak and faint, but I rushed over to her bedside.

"Did you call for me?" I asked. The candle was still flickering. She had not gotten up to blow it out, and I wondered if she even had the strength to.

She lay in bed, staring at the ceiling. Her skin looked clammy and white. "Yes."

"Do you need some water or something cool for your head?"

She looked agonized and just choked out, "No."

"Do you need me to just sit here with you?"

She nodded and there was a pause. "I need you to finish your story."

I stared at her. I didn't know what to say. "You know what happens next," I said.

She nodded. "She was whipped for dropping the china. My mother's china."

The stillness of that moment. The hot tears that escaped from my eyes. I remembered Chloe. I remembered her panic as Mrs. Caroline yelled at her for destroying the china. Chloe begged, as Mrs. Caroline yelled for her brother Charles to come downstairs and to handle this complete lack of care. Master Marshall hadn't even had a moment to come and process his sister's arrival. Many people did not even know that this was his sister. I didn't know at the time. But Chloe knew and she said in haste, "Little Miss Marshall, I am so sorry. I will-"

"You'll what?! You'll pay for it? How will you pay for it?" she had said.

Master Marshall answered for her. "She'll pay for it with stripes."

Chloe sobbed and begged. I sobbed and begged. You even tried to convince him that maybe that wasn't necessary, but you had already done the damage. I even offered to take the stripes for Chloe. Master Marshall would have none of it. He whipped Chloe in front of us. An old woman.

When it was over, Chloe laid limp and lifeless. Her head bowed; her body now was nothing more than a shell.

"I heard what you said that day," I said. "Charles, I can't believe you and mama kept her here after she brought Azariah back here. Perhaps it was for the best. If it wasn't for her, Daddy would still be alive."

She didn't respond to me at first. She only turned on her side and faced the candle, watching it burn. "Finish your story," she commanded, her back still to me. When she heard no response, I heard her weakly say, "Please, Naima."

I didn't want to talk anymore. I thought it about what it might look like to just leave her here and let her waste away on her own. I found myself angry that I hadn't killed her before. There were plenty of opportunities to. I don't know if she deserved to hear my story. But I found myself continuing.

***

October 1861. That's when everything changed. Two years after I arrived at Red Oaks.

We already lived in terror with just Master Marshall, and now that you were back, it was worse. Both of you were on a mission to obtain revenge. You wanted revenge for your father, and he wanted retribution for his mother's reputation.

Master Marshall did not allow church services, and now I understood why. Master Marshall could not risk what had happened years before. Not if he wanted to maintain power here. People gathered in secret to share just bits of gospel truth that they knew.

The next night, I went out for a walk, praying as I walked, "And he said unto me, my grace is sufficient for thee: for my strength is made perfect in weakness. Most gladly therefore will I rather glory in my infirmities, that the power of Christ may rest upon me. Therefore, I take pleasure in infirmities, in reproaches, in necessities, in persecutions, in distresses for Christ's sake: for when I am weak, then am I strong."

"Talking to yourself?"

I heard his voice behind me. I stilled, but did not turn around. I could hear his footsteps walking to my side, and then he stepped in front of me. His blond hair looked darker to me than before, and he towered over me with his hard green eyes. I was twenty years old at this point, and I knew that Charles was more than double my age.

"I asked you a question. Who are you talking to?"

"To God," I said. "I was remembering a scripture. I was praying."

"Praying?" he said incredulously.

"Before I came here, I often attended church, read the Word, and prayed."

"What do you pray for?" he asked me.

I didn't know what to say. I hadn't been expecting him to ask me something like this. "It depends. Sometimes I pray for simple things, like for a peaceful rest, and sometimes I pray for bigger things."

"Like what?" he asked gruffly.

"Sometimes I pray for strength, for peace,

for joy."

"Does he give it to you?"

"Yes," I said, "Yes, he does."

He seemed to relax and gave me some physical space as he thought for a moment. "Well, if he hears you, then pray he gives it to me too."

I should've remained silent, but foolishly I asked, "What will you use it for?"

He cocked his head, and he looked as if he might strike me, but instead he said, "Mind yourself."

I nodded. "My apologies, I will pray for you Master Marshall."

I hoped that I was being dismissed so I slowly moved to walk away and head back to my cabin and he stopped me. "Naima, just a reminder that you are not to gather with others to pray."

"Yes, sir."

"I was aware that when you were brought to us, you had been living in the North, and you know how to read."

I wanted to say, "Do you mean when I had been free?", but instead, I just said "Yes, sir"

"If I ever see you showing others to read, so help me, I will whip you within an inch of your life and sell you to a brothel if I can."

His threat filled me with fear, but also with fury that he had the audacity to fully believe that he was in control over my body and soul. "Yes, sir. I have never openly read in front of anyone."

"Good," he said, and then he reached for my hand. "There was a negress that I once enjoyed, and I must say, even though you are a handful, you are even more intriguing and attractive than she was. Join me in my quarters tonight."

I recoiled and pulled my hand from him. "Please, Master Marshall, I beg you not to do this."

He shushed me. "Naima, I do not need to, but I am asking kindly."

I closed my eyes and prayed inwardly. *Lord, give me the words to say.* "If you are asking, that would imply that I have a choice. Master

Marshall, I would like to go back to my cabin and pray for you in earnest. Or we can remain out here and talk if you wish."

He stared at me. "You are an insolent wench." He stepped forward towards me, and I braced myself, keeping my head down.

"I am sorry, sir. I do not mean to be rude. I only mean to be a chaste young woman. However, if you wish to have me keep you company, I do not mind, sir."

"Keep me company?"

"Yes, your role here on the plantation must be a lonely one at times. Everyone needs someone to talk to, even you."

He seemed to be again stunned by my answer and laughed. "You are something else, Naima. Something else…" he said as his voice trailed off. "You seem to be fairly smart. I suppose talking to you would be… interesting."

I released a breath I had not been aware that I was holding in. "May I ask you a question, sir?"

"You may."

"Why do you not allow the slaves to gather to pray or to attend church?"

He stared up at the night sky and then put his head down and spat on the ground. "One of my father's slaves, long ago, when I was a child, came with his prophesies and what not. He beguiled him, and my *weak* father gave up everything to follow that ape's words." His voice started to rise in anger, his words chopped and biting. "It cost me and my family everything. The fortune wasn't even the worst of the devastation, but it was the fact that he freed every monkey on this plantation that ruined our family name. It took me *years* to build back this place and our family name."

I chose my words carefully. "How did you manage?"

"My mother was what held us together. She knew that my father had made a mistake, and she didn't let us get led away by his foolishness. There were some of the slaves that had stayed behind. They thought that my father's delusions that they were free meant something to us. So, my mother made sure that they understood their place. Even though the whole community had turned their backs on us because of my father, she remarried, and her husband helped her set this place back in order, and when I was old enough, she made sure that everything was passed on to me."

"Is your mother still alive?"

"No, she passed on about 5 years ago."

"I am sorry for your loss."

"Are you truly?" he said to me. I could tell that he was earnest, yet still guarded and suspicious.

"I am. I understand loss and I understand rejection."

He seemed to want to come back with a retort but decided against it. "Man, that is born of a woman is of few days and full of trouble."

"Amen," I said. "But there is hope."

"Hope…" he said, looking up at the sky. "I have done everything that I once hoped for. Now, I can eat, drink and be merry."

"Luke 12," I said.

"I'm sorry, what did you say?"

"Luke 12. You said eat, drink and be merry. It's from Luke 12."

I couldn't tell if he was annoyed or intrigued. I often couldn't tell if he was annoyed or intrigued by me. Perhaps it was a mix of both. I knew that he desired me yet felt disgusted that he desired me.

"How do you just remember that?" he asked me.

"Master Marshall, you have many slaves on this plantation, and you can remember all of our names. How do you do that?"

"I must remember your names if I am to manage you. You are my bread and butter."

"Even though I have not been able to read God's Word since I've come here, I meditate on it every day. It is my daily bread."

"Does it give you hope?"

"Yes, it gives me hope that he is here with me."

He thought for a moment. "Yes, well then, I am glad that you hope to remain here where he is with you. I would hate for you to turn out like your mother and father."

"Neither would I." I know that he meant that he would hate for me to run away and for him to have to punish me, but I meant that I would live my life apart from Christ and to die apart from him as well.

"Luke 12," he said, "I may have to go back and find that scripture. Will you come back to my quarters with me to find it?"

"Are you permitting me to read?" I said, looking him in the eye. I knew that this was forbidden, but I wanted to make sure that I could read his facial expressions clearly.

"I am permitting you to read to me tonight."

"Only to read?"

He glared at me. "Only to read," he said. "For just tonight."

I nodded. "Yes, I will join you in your quarters to *just* read."

He thought that my focus was on reading, but my focus was on him not wanting anything else. In his ignorance he responded. "For tonight," he said.

"Yes, sir, I understand."

He walked ahead of me as I followed about two paces behind him. When we approached the house and made our way up the stairs, I could see some of the women who worked in the home staring at me, some in concern for my wellbeing, some in jealousy that they thought this was some social status that I enjoyed. When we passed by you, you grabbed his arm and said, "For someone who so despises our father, you seem to have his same appetite."

He slapped you and told you to shut up and your husband peeked out and saw you holding your cheek. He was alarmed and about to defend you.

Master Marshall just said, "When you have your own place to stay, then you can dictate what happens on your property, with your property. You are lucky that I am letting you stay here," he said to him. "Especially after your betrayal, Caroline," he said to you.

It was the only time I felt the smallest bit of sadness for you. I was grateful that he did not lead me into his bedroom and instead into his study.

There were a few small candles lit in there, but the room was too dark for reading. It was then that I saw it. The candlestick. He lit a large pillar candle that was already on it. The top of the candle was already warped because it had been lit before. Then he went to his bookcase and retrieved a Bible that looked as though it had never been touched.

"Find the scripture," he commanded, as he handed me the Bible and sat in his chair behind his desk.

My eyes laid fixed on the candlestick.

"What are you staring at?" he asked with annoyance.

"I'm sorry, sir, it's just that you have a beautiful candlestick."

He rolled his eyes. "This old piece of junk. With its stupid lore. My father swore that this thing brought his family fortune throughout the generations."

"Then why do you keep it if you do not believe?"

He chuckled. "Because Caroline wants it. You know how it is. Sibling rivalry."

"I have no siblings."

"Lucky you." He rested his elbows on his desk. "My father never lit a candle on it. Swore that it couldn't be lit again, or some bad omen would happen. It's just all nonsense. My fortune has only increased since I lit this candle. The day I lit it, we found your mother and father…and you."

I stood there, heat rushing through my body, I could hear my own heart beating.

"Go ahead, read it to me. Luke 12."

I looked back down at the Bible in my hands. It had been two years since I last read a Bible. A part of me wanted to grab it and run, so that I could just read and read. My soul was thirsty for it. I turned to Luke 12 and looked for the right scriptures and began to read.

"And one of the company said unto him, Master,

speak to my brother, that he divide the inheritance with me. And he said unto him, Man, who made me a judge or a divider over you? And he said unto them, Take heed, and beware of covetousness: for a man's life consisteth not in the abundance of the things which he possesseth. And he spake a parable unto them, saying, The ground of a certain rich man brought forth plentifully: And he thought within himself, saying, What shall I do, because I have no room where to bestow my fruits? And he said, This will I do: I will pull down my barns, and build greater; and there will I bestow all my fruits and my goods. And I will say to my soul, Soul, thou hast much goods laid up for many years; take thine ease, eat, drink, and be merry. But God said unto him, Thou fool, this night thy soul shall be required of thee: then whose shall those things be, which thou hast provided? So is he that layeth up treasure for himself, and is not rich toward God."

I looked up and noticed that he was staring intensely at me. "You think I am the fool in the story."

"I merely remembered that you had said the same very words of this scripture."

"Will my life be demanded of me this very

night?" he asked, his voice on edge.

I took a deep breath. *Lord, give me guidance.* I looked down at the opened page and saw: *And I say unto you my friends, be not afraid of them that kill the body, and after that have no more that they can do. But I will forewarn you whom ye shall fear: Fear him, which after he hath killed hath power to cast into hell; yea, I say unto you, Fear him.*

I took a deep breath, and I finally responded. "Only if the Lord wishes for it to be so."

"God is no different than me then. He kills when he is angry. He kills if his property does not obey."

I stepped forward to him. "May I show you another scripture?"

He eyed me warily again. "You may."

I wondered if I would remember the verse, there were so many times I had gone to this scripture asking for the Lord to show patience towards my parents. *Lord help me to remember the scripture.*

I flipped the pages and then it came to me,

and I turned the pages in haste. Exodus 34:6-7. "The LORD, The LORD God, merciful and gracious, longsuffering, and abundant in goodness and truth, keeping mercy for thousands, forgiving iniquity and transgression and sin, and that will by no means clear the guilty; visiting the iniquity of the fathers upon the children, and upon the children's children, unto the third and forth generation."

He looked from me and then at the page skeptically. "Explain it to me," he said.

"This is the first time in the Bible that God himself describes who he is, what his character is like."

He still looked at me with confusion. "He enjoys punishing generations."

"No, sir. He first describes himself as merciful and gracious, patient, abundant in goodness and truth. He forgives sin. But he does not let the guilty go unpunished." I still sensed his leeriness and asked. "May I borrow your candle?"

"What?"

"Your candle."

"I know what a candle is. What does it have to do with the scripture?"

"You asked me to explain the scripture. I hope to give an example."

Yet again, I could not tell if he was angry with me, fascinated by me, in disbelief, or in wonder. He handed me the whole candlestick with the candle still burning on it, its wax dripping down the side of it.

"Think of it as this: we all have a candle, our lifespan, a measure of grace given to us that we do not deserve. The flame is God's wrath for sin, all sin, our sin. Left unchecked the flame will continue to burn, melting away at our time, at the measure of grace for our lives. The Lord is patient with our disobedience to his Word because He loves us. He will forgive our sins, out the flame of wrath to come, but only if we let him."

"How do we let him? Does God come down and out this supposed flame?"

"He did. Jesus took the wrath of God on

himself for the sins of humanity. But most of us try to hide that there is a flame at all, we pretend that God is ignorant of our sin. But the flame and the candle of wax go hand in hand. Just as God's justice and his kindness do too. He can't be fully kind, without being committed to justice. So even God's wrath is beautiful, just as this flame is beautiful, it gives us a light to see in the dark, warmth for the coldest of nights. But, just like this beautiful, light filled, warm flame, God's grace and patience does come to the end of the candlestick, and it has the potential to burn this place."

His eyes searched mine with suspicion, and he breathed deeply. "Go on."

"We must acknowledge that we need help to put out the flame. Here's what Jesus does," I said, as I blew the flame out.

"All he does is blow the flame out?" He said, as he laughed. "I can do that myself."

"All sin must be atoned for with the blood of something spotless, perfect, sinless. You are a sinful man. You cannot satisfy the wrath of

God."

He leaned back in his chair pensively. "So am I the sinner and you the saint?"

"Do you mean, do I think that I am better than you? No. I am a sinner, through and through. My sins are so many that I cannot name them all." The number of times I've thought about murdering him alone would be enough sin for a lifetime.

I continued, "But I have turned away from my sin. I want them no more. I accept that Jesus alone, the only sinless person could atone for me on the cross. He blew my candle out years ago."

He got up from his seat and started to walk towards me. "You remind me of Azariah, that deceiver, who once lived here on this plantation. The same liar that came and cast some spell on my father and got him to turn this place into a mockery."

He stepped forward and grabbed my jaw forcefully. "So, when I tell you that I won't allow some *witch* to come in and charm your way into doing the same. Don't give me your candle analogies, or your words pleading for me to repent, because I have *nothing* to repent of. You people were born beneath me and will remain beneath me," he said, as he released me. My face radiated with pain. As he grabbed me for the first time since my parents had passed, I felt it happening again. I felt the Lord's words burning in my chest, burning as they traveled to my throat. I tried to hold them back because I knew that this word could be the death of me.

He glared at me. "Cat got your tongue this time?"

I thought about resisting the Lord. It could save my life. Then I remembered Paul's words. To live is Christ and to die is gain. I had already lost everything. To be home with my Lord would be better than this. *Lord, I am yours. Speak through me.* "No," I said. "I have not come to plead with you to repent."

He narrowed his eyes. "Yet, I know you have something to say."

I don't know how I managed to do it, but I squared my soldiers and said to him plainly.

"He has sent me here not to plead with you to repent, but to give you judgment."

"Judgment?" he growled.

"Your candle wick is growing shorter by the day. One day it will burn, and this whole kingdom you have built will be nothing but ashes and ruins."

"You amuse me, Naima," he said, as he sat back on his chair. He pointed his hand for me to sit in another chair opposite of him. "You come to me with judgment, but what about your God of love and justice?"

I wanted to remain standing to remain prepared in case he chose to attack me, but I obeyed and sat. "I told you before, God is holy. For him to be love and to uphold justice, then he must hate what is evil. He cannot just pardon it."

"You have mighty fine language for a tar baby, let alone a woman. Who taught you all these words like 'justice' and 'pardon'? Shouldn't you have been practicing knowing how to cook? Well, what about Jesus? You told me he forgives sins. Can't I just wait for the moment before I die, and then I ask for forgiveness?"

I thought about his words, considered them, chewed on them. "Yes, Jesus does forgive…. but God has not merely pardoned sin. He still punished for sin. He accepted a substitute. Jesus. For he hath made him *to be* sin for us, who knew no sin; that we might be made the righteousness of God in him. You must believe on Jesus to be saved."

"I believe in Jesus."

"What has Jesus saved you from?"

He looked confused and then angry. "You're trying to trick me."

"I am not."

"You're trying to do the same thing my father did. Try to convince me that there's something wrong with me." He stalked about and then slammed his hand against the wall, "Well ain't nothing wrong with me! Something was wrong with him for thinking that it was a good idea to free you animals. Jesus ain't never said anything about you slaves and across the Bible there's proof that I'm supposed to rule over you. You see, people who love God keep things in his natural order, the way he wants to keep things going."

He did not understand. "No," I said, shaking my head. "What do you believe about God? What do you believe about Jesus? What do you believe about who he is?"

"Enough questions, Naima!"

"Is he love? Is he holy? Is he justice? Who is he?"

"I am your God!" he said as he screamed in my face, his spit spraying on me. "You obey me! You are property! Nothing more!"

"Because of your greed that's why you choose to negate everything you see about me. You see that I am just like you. I am made by God, I speak, I feel. That's why you still feel attracted to me. I am not an animal."

"I have been too loose with you, letting you run your mouth like this to me."

I continued with tears in my eyes. "Growing up, I thought God was dealing so harshly with my parents. I was angry that he was treating them with the same judgment as people like you. But now I see why. They were just like you. All your life God has tried to tell you who he is, to show you through the transformed life of your father, he has been patient with you, but your heart is hard and will not turn to God, because you believe that you *are* God. That you can determine who is worth living and dying, that you can determine what is right and wrong. God's grace and patience with you should compel you to seek him, but instead, you see it as permission to do as you please. So, your empty prayer to him moments before you die, will not be received, because it is not with words, but with the heart that one repents. Just as your father repented. You had a chance to follow in the footsteps of your father. But you chose to multiply his evil. The cries of God's people have risen to him, and it has not gone unnoticed. So thus, saith the Lord, *Behold, I am against thee, saith the Lord of hosts, and I will burn your chariots in the smoke, and the sword shall devour thy young lions: and I will cut off thy prey from the earth, and the voice of thy messengers shall no more be heard."*

This time he did not laugh. He dealt with me so severely that I could not work for days, but I made sure that even amidst the pain, as he walked away from me, I gave him the final message I had been given from the Lord.

And it shall come to pass, that all they that look upon thee shall flee from thee, and say, Marshall is laid waste: who will bemoan him? Whence shall I seek comforters for thee?

When I woke up, I was back in Chloe's old cabin. I was delirious and dreamt she was still there with me. Humming her songs. When I came to, I realized that there was pain all over and instead it was just Olive.

"Rest," she said.

I lay back on the bed. "How long have I been here?"

"Two days."

I closed my eyes.

"What happened, Naima?" she asked.

I opened my eyes and tried to sit up again. "I am fine. Go prepare yourselves," I said trying to get up. "Judgment is coming."

"You're not well," she said. "You need to lie back down."

"I do not know how it will come or when it will come. But I do know that this time, when it does, you and I will be free. Go! Prepare yourself."

***

Once my body had healed, I returned to work and Master Marshall avoided me. I was grateful for that. He had been busy at work to acquire another plantation and "expand his empire". He had finally succeeded and decided to throw a raucous party. He had sent out invitations telling everyone "To eat, drink, and be merry."

Attendees were drinking so much that they began to stumble around, sloshing their whiskey across the floor. The place reeked of liquor and cigarettes. There were couples, unmarried, doing things that I will not detail. Master Marshall had instructed men from all over which of the enslaved women here that they could enjoy as they pleased. Master Marshall had allowed every evil to come into this place. You were there, Mrs. Caroline. You saw it all. My heart was sick with disgust, my heart was sick with grief at this sin.

As I served the guests additional food, across the parlor, I saw Master Marshall come in unsteadily from outside. He was carrying the candlestick, and he yelled at you. You were watching him closely, and then he tumbled inside, and the candle fell to the ground and suddenly the ground was ablaze and the laughter inside turned into screams. Most of us tried to help put out the fire, but instead were met with drunken stupor. I realized something in the moment as I watched these men and women reject our pleas to help them get to safety. Their greed for power and money was like the whiskey they loved. The more they had, the less they had the ability to reason, and like this fire, their greed burned them alive. The hatred they had for us led them to reject our help. Their sin consumed them. Their wax was down to its last drop. And you, I watched you. You watched him burn…with gladness as you picked up the candlestick.

Your brother's eyes were frenzied as he tried to save his precious plantation to no avail. The wind suddenly picked up outside, and I knew that the Lord was allowing this whirlwind to come and consume this place. I watched as the flames caught his shirt sleeve and traveled across his body as he screamed and flailed. He had no thought to repent as he supposed he would. There was no time to think of that amidst his panic and pain. I scurried to help him, grabbing something to beat away the flames. He recoiled from my gracious offering. His screams filled not just my ears, but every fiber of my being, and I desperately tried to help him. But, I realized as the wind whipped around me, that it was useless. There was no water around to oust him and when everything was done, the only thing left to describe the Red Oaks: the place where blood from the whip had soaked the ground, where families were torn apart from each other, where women could find no safe meadow, and where Marshall had built his throne, was forever remembered as nothing more than mere ashes. *Thou fool, this night thy soul shall be required of thee.*

***

When I finished telling my story, I didn't know what I expected from Mrs. Caroline. No, I think that I was expecting her anger. Anger that I would tell this story of destruction about her beloved plantations and Southern lifestyle. Anger that I would accuse her of reveling in her brother's death. I was so used to her disdain or indifference that I wasn't expecting her frail hand on mine.

"I'm sorry," she said, and patted my hand.

I thought about telling her that nothing could erase the suffering that I had endured and the suffering of Chloe, my mother, father, and all those who lived with me and before me, but as I looked into her eyes, welling up with tears, I could sense her genuine sorrow.

I felt the pull of anger seeing her tears. The urge to smother her in her weak state appeared. *Lord, help me*, I prayed internally. Then unexpectedly, tears started to escape mine as well. I started to swipe at them quickly, afraid to show any vulnerability and then I felt her hand on my cheek, wiping away a tear as well.

She put her arm down. "I am an evil woman. I promised myself I would never be like my mother, twisted and bent by bitterness." She scoffed. "But I am my mother's child." She wiped at her face. "What I did to Chloe is unforgiveable. What I let him do to you…" Her chin trembled.

"Why did you come back?"

Her voice was shaky as she spoke, "When my father got the message from Azariah, he called us all into a fast. We were supposed to pray for forgiveness. He spoke to me and explained to me that what we did on the plantation was wicked. I didn't understand. All my life, this was normal. The people on the plantation were barely even human, they were made for this. So, I did what I thought was best. I played along. I pretended to be transformed."

I sighed and looked down and then I looked back at her wanting her to continue.

"He was so happy. He just seemed relieved that I was on the right path, and he was agonized at the condition of my mother and brother. He changed his will, and he passed everything down to me, and his most prized possession: that golden candlestick. It was worth a fortune. But my mother believed in the tale and never wanted to sell it. She believed that if they hung on to it, it's magic would bring us fortune again. My mother and my brother tried hard to ensure that I would be willing to run this place like it once was. But even though I didn't agree with my father, I wanted to honor his wishes and make sure this place wasn't filled with…violence anymore. They tried to kill me. With poison. But it didn't work. So, I left, and my mother moved on."

"She married again?"

"Yes. When my father passed, my mother was so angry. It…. consumed her." She wiped her tears away weakly. "Before he died, I think that she would've wanted more than anything for him to love her. My father was good to me, but even I knew that he was not a good husband. He talked to her like she was nothing and then there were the mulattoes, quadroons, and octaroons everywhere. When I was young, I didn't quite understand, but when I got older…" She trailed off and then cleared her throat. "I think I was the only one grieving for him when he died. My mother was so grateful when she met Mr. Reed. He was just what she needed, an older man just grateful that she would look his way."

"My mother?" I asked. "What happened with my mother?"

"Your mother was like a sister to me." She cleared her throat. "She was my sister." She sounded like she could barely talk. "I didn't want to believe that he had done that to her. I should've believed her. Nothing was the same after that. Not with her, nor with him. Even after we got married and moved North."

"And Chloe?"

She covered her face now completely and started to sob. "I didn't think he was going to do that! Chloe was mine; he had no right."

"Chloe was not your property!"

She stared into my eyes. "Chloe was more of a mother to me than my own. Chloe nursed me."

I felt the weight of my fury begin to weigh down on me. How could people convince themselves that another person was subhuman, yet give their child to be suckled by someone they considered an animal? I could only conclude that they knew all too well that these were humans but needed to justify their evil. If I stayed here, I would kill her. With my bare hands.

"You told me why you left. Not why you came back." I lost control and screamed in her face, my spit landing on her.

"Answer me!"

Mrs. Caroline surprisingly shrunk back. "My husband and I had enough money to come back and to take it by force if necessary. But I needed to come and have my brother trust me, and then I could strike and take back this plantation."

"So, you had enough money for your own home?"

She nodded. "But I needed to be in the home. I wanted to be there." She swallowed. "I did not know that he was like my father in that way and for that too, I am desperately sorry. I understand all too well the violation," she said, "I fought so hard for that plantation, for that home. It burned to the ground, and I didn't get any of it. All I had was the candlestick."

I looked over to her side and saw the candlestick there with its burning candle. She continued, "We bought another home, and we were doing well." Her chin trembled again. "When the Union soldiers came, they found me in my home and my husband was away at war.

There were many of them." Her whole body trembled, as she fought to control her tears. "I thought I wouldn't survive. Months later when my husband returned from the war, he returned and found me round with a child. After years of what I thought was barrenness, I was pregnant with a Union soldier's child. I told him everything and I don't know if it was because he doubted my faithfulness, felt shame at his own impotence, or if he was disgusted with me, but he would barely look at me after that. I stayed faithful to him all those years even though he never had and, in my distress, he turned his back on me."

For the first time ever, I think I saw Mrs. Caroline. Now, I understood her cause. "So, you started the organization."

"Yes. After my son was born, I was struggling to bond with him, but then I realized with my husband's feelings towards me, my son was all that I had. I started to look around and I realized other women around had similar stories. The Union took everything from us. The money we could recover from, but they took our safety, our security, our dignity." She looked over and pointed at the candlestick. "All this time, I thought that candlestick would bring me fortune, and instead it has brought my family nothing but pain."

I looked at it. "You all have looked to everything to bring you peace but God. Your golden candlestick is nothing more than a golden calf."

"Sell it and keep the money, Naima."

The choice that lay before me was the hardest that I had to make thus far. "May I read something to you?" I asked.

She nodded; I reached for the Bible in her room. "The Lord is slow to anger, and great in power, and will not at all acquit the wicked: the Lord hath his way in the whirlwind and in the storm, and the clouds are the dust of his feet," I set the Bible aside, "No, one gets away with anything."

She closed her eyes and breathed. "Forgive us," she said. "Forgive me."

I could not speak. Never in my years had I imagined these words would come from any Southern man or woman. I cleared my throat and fought back the burning and stinging of tears. "Father, forgive them, they know not what they do."

"I did." she said. "I did understand. I deserve the guilt. I saw everything. I saw the brutality and the violations, and I did nothing. I told myself that it could not be wrong if everyone believes it to be right. I told myself it must not be wrong if God did not stop it. I was so foolish and filled with pride. Now, I am dying and there's no way to undo what I have done, what I have condoned, what I have *championed*." she said with such desperation in her voice.

"I know," I said. "I know."

"God forgive me," she said, pitifully. "I do not deserve for you to stay here with me as I die."

Many will not forgive me for what comes next.

Did she deserve it? No, I do not feel that

she does. I wanted so badly to get up and walk out of the room and leave her in her misery. I could head up North and walk away from her forever. I could be a rich woman from the gold. My ears felt warm, and my eyes were burning. The curse and cycle had to be broken.

"I forgive you," I said. Then the tears finally began to pour out of me, and I wept more than I had since I lost my mother and father. I had not realized that even in my silent servitude, the weight of anger and pain left my heart completely weak.

"I would've given anything for my mother and father to have done this when they were in their last moments. Anything. I know they had done evil, and I didn't care if they made it in by the skin of their teeth. I just wanted them to repent. I know you don't feel like you deserve my forgiveness, and maybe you don't, I don't know. I don't understand a lot of things, Mrs. Caroline. But I do understand that God is gracious to me and will be to you. I am not leaving you alone to die," I said.

I spent the first eighteen years of my life having never known the bondage of slavery, but for the first time, I felt freedom. I thought I was chosen for the judgment that fell on the Marshall Plantation. But now, I realized that I was chosen for *this* moment.

It was then that she sobbed, blubbering, until she went into a fit of coughing. I held her hand tightly, and she gave me the softest smile and then gave up the ghost. I let go of her hand, took a deep breath, and the candle at her bedside suddenly flickered out. There was darkness all around. It took a bit for my eyes to adjust, but once it did, I stopped and stared at the candle, on that golden candlestick. I moved to touch the candlestick and noticed that even though the candle was almost all gone, there was faintest bit of wax left behind.

ABOUT THE AUTHOR

Shaida Escoffery Whitley is the author of several books including *Idle, Wild, Love*, *The Children of Eden*, and *Bloom*. Born in Brooklyn, NY and raised in Miami, FL, she is the alumna of the University of Miami, where she received the Atlantic Coast Conference's Innovation and Creativity Fellowship for her work on *Idle, Wild, Love*. She is also a graduate of New York University's Graduate School. Since graduating, she has worked as a dedicated schoolteacher and serves her local church in discipleship and worship. She currently resides in Miami, FL with her husband, Micah and their daughter Brielle.

Coming July 2025